DEMON NIGHT

THE RESURRECTION CHRONICLES

M.J. HAAG

To my readers who continue to support my work with each purchase,
Thank you and here's another one!

To readers who download books from non-pay, non-library sites,
It's called book piracy. It's illegal. Don't do it.

Every secret has a price.

It's a truth that Angel knows too well. Since the hellhounds and infected started to roam, Angel has guarded her secret carefully. But, she's growing weaker by the day and needs help. In this new plague-ravaged world, the weak don't survive long, and the useless are quickly abandoned. That's why Angel's secret needs to stay secret. If anyone found out about the baby she carried, they'd ditch her in a heartbeat to save themselves.

To make herself an asset, she offers her services as a relationship expert to one of the dark fey, who rose with the hellhounds, in exchange for food. Shax is eager to win over Hannah, and if Angel can help make that happen, just maybe she won't be kicked out of the settlement when she has the baby.

WHAT HAS HAPPENED BEFORE...

More than two months ago, earthquakes unleashed hellhounds on an unsuspecting mankind. The bite of a hound changes humans, turning people into flesh-craving infected. The hellhounds weren't the only things to emerge from the earthen caverns. Demon men with grey skin and reptilian eyes have been trapped underground for thousands of years. They alone can kill the hellhounds and help bring a stop to the plague. They only ask for one thing in return: a chance to meet women who might be willing to love them as they are.

CHAPTER ONE

I RAN THROUGH THE SURVIVOR CAMP WITH EVERY OUNCE OF energy I had, one human in a herd of humans, trying to escape the infected. The people around me were screaming and yelling, making it harder to hear what was behind us. I didn't try to look. I already knew what the infected looked like. Pale. Cloudy eyes. Missing parts. A craving for human flesh.

A woman tripped on a tent stake and fell in front of me. If I had been a better person, I would have stopped and tried to help her up. But I didn't. I couldn't. I'd promised I would do everything in my power to survive. So, I kept running even as I cramped. Even as every breath sent a stab of pain through my middle.

You can do this, Angel.

Because, I knew if I couldn't, I would die.

Out of nowhere, a fey came running at me.

"Get down!" he yelled.

I fell to my stomach and winced at the wet splattering sound behind me.

"Run," he said.

I hopped to my feet, almost slipping on infected blood slicking the snow around me, and ran again. I knew my clothing was covered in infected blood but didn't stop to remove any of the seven layers.

Ahead, I spotted the hangar. A beacon of safety.

I made it through the door with several other winded runners. A crowd of people had already gathered inside. We were cattle waiting for the slaughter if the fey couldn't keep up with the infected pouring into the safe zone.

One of the grey devils strode past as I walked small circles, trying to cool down from the mad sprint to the hangar. The fey—tall, broad-shouldered, and all males— appeared after the earthquakes that were felt around the world weeks ago. If they were the only things to appear, humanity would have been fine. But they weren't. And now, humanity was struggling to exist. Honestly though, humanity wasn't putting up much of a struggle. We were a pathetically weak lot in comparison to what was now out there. The fey were huge, strong, and liked ripping heads off of things, but they had a soft spot for women. Thankfully. Human men they only tolerated.

Too bad the hellhounds came before the fey.

Unable to bear the pain in my middle for a moment longer, I braced my hands on my knees and hoped that belly dive hadn't hurt the baby. I had landed mostly on my knees and elbows, and at just six months pregnant, I didn't have much of a bump, yet.

Please, just stay where you are, I thought to my stowaway. *Now is not the time for a surprise appearance.*

Not that I thought a few more weeks would make the world a safer place. Today. Tomorrow. Nine weeks from now. The length of time didn't change the truth of our situation. This baby and I were royally fucked.

"Angel, are you okay?" Matt Davis asked.

I straightened to look at the man who led our sad excuse for a safe zone. But, since it was the only safe zone left, it was also the most shining example.

"Yeah. Fine. Avoided being future fertilizer, thanks to one of the fey." I tried to straighten but winced at the pain that speared through my side. Replacing my hands on my knees, I resumed my study of the floor.

Matt gently curled a hand around my arm and led me to the wall where other people were sitting.

"I sent one of the fey for Mrs. Felds. Sit. Yell if you need something."

I nodded and sank to the cement floor. It didn't matter that it was cold; it wasn't outside with the infected.

"Bertha," Matt called. "Get Angel a juice. Her blood sugar is dropping again."

I set my head on my knees rather than look at the accusing stares of the people around me. I didn't have a problem with blood sugar. Matt knew that. He also knew I didn't want anyone to find out about the baby. The earthquakes, hellhounds, and the spread of the zombie-like plague had changed the benevolent nature of the people who remained. Who was I kidding? Benevolence died out long before the quakes. If people found out I was pregnant, that there'd soon be another mouth needing a share of rations, I'd find myself on the wrong side of the fence.

"Here," a familiar, brusque voice said.

I looked up and took the small bottle of juice that Bertha held out. The woman was more sour than a bunch of green grapes.

"Thanks," I said with my best namesake smile.

"Sip it slowly. If it doesn't help, there's not much I can do. That's out of the doc's fridge. All the supplies are—" She looked in the direction of the door, and I understood. No one would be eating anything until the fey cleared the latest breach in the fence.

She moved away, and I cracked open the bottle to take a cautious sip. When I did, I saw the blood coating my sleeve. The reminder of just how close that infected had been hit me hard. I was getting slower. Too slow.

Shaking, I set down the bottle and peeled off my outermost layer of clothing.

"I'll take that," Matt said, moving to squat in front of me. "You sure you're okay?"

I nodded even though I wasn't at all sure. I didn't want him to worry about me, though. Matt had enough on his plate. Okay, fine, I didn't give a shit about his plate. I just didn't want him to call any more attention to me.

"The juice is already working its magic," I said.

He patted my knee, took the bloody jacket, and walked away.

Outside, the sounds of fighting grew louder. Instead of paying attention to that, I tried to subtly rub my stomach. It was hard as a rock, aching, and freaking me the fuck out. Touching it didn't help.

Feeling light-headed and a bit queasy, I gave up on rubbing and just rested my hands on my knees.

"Come on, give a girl a break," I whispered.

I thought of Mrs. Felds, Whiteman's previous camp doctor by default, and wished for the millionth time she had remembered to have someone take me back to Tolerance when the fey had delivered the supplies a few days ago.

"This isn't right," someone said lowly.

I almost lifted my head, thinking that the speaker meant what was going on in the hangar.

"The doc should be here."

I barely contained a snort. News of Mrs. Felds' leaving hadn't gone over well with some. Even though the woman was no actual doctor, people here still felt she owed them something. That she'd chosen to go live with the fey at Tolerance rather than stay in Whiteman was beyond their understanding. But, why the hell would she want to stay where the infected kept getting in? I sure as hell didn't.

"I heard she went out and found her son and another survivor. Took them back to Tolerance," someone else said.

"Good," another said. "Last thing we need is more mouths to feed."

The sentiment made my belly clench tighter even as someone else made a sound of disbelief.

"We need all the people we can get," the original speaker said. "There's not enough of us to guard the fence the way it is. Why do you think the infected breached it? Either someone missed their shift or fell asleep on it. We're all overworked and pulling too many doubles."

"Fine. The last thing we need is more useless mouths to feed," the other speaker amended. "A baby isn't going to do jack to keep us alive."

I clenched my hands into fists and kept quiet. This was an argument I'd heard since the moment there were whispers about food shortages, and it was the main reason I didn't want anyone to know I was pregnant.

"How could a single person with an infant even survive outside the fence?" the original speaker asked. "We can barely survive in here."

He was right. A human outside the fence was as good as dead. Heck, living inside the fence was risky, now. I'd seen more than one survivor crossed off the list on my run to the hangar.

Whiteman's fences weren't enough to keep us safe anymore. It didn't take a genius to figure out the fey were the key to surviving or that Matt's biggest mistake had been treating the fey like workhorses. The fey might have been able to do all the tasks, but overworked and underappreciated people rarely hung around. With the fey now living in Tolerance, Whiteman was just an infecteds' supermarket, and we humans were the deli.

If Mrs. Felds didn't take me with her today, I didn't think I'd live through another attack. Hell, I shouldn't have made it to the hangar during this one.

I took a sip of juice, and a little of the precious liquid dribbled down my chin because of my unsteady hand. Even though I'd caught my breath and the pain in my side had eased, the shaking wasn't letting up. I had almost died, spared by chance within the last half a second. That I was an out of shape, underfed pregnant woman who'd just sprinted a mile didn't help me feel any better about anything.

Someone pounded on the outer door, a heavy thud that echoed through the hangar. The murmured conversations hushed slightly, allowing me to hear a muted voice yelling Matt Davis' name.

"That can't be good," one of the people sitting near me said.

I lifted my head just as the door opened, and a fey strode in carrying Mrs. Felds. Relief coursed through me, and I put my head down again. The doctor was here. Finally.

As soon as I could stop shaking, I'd track her down and talk to her. Remind her of her promise that I could live at Tolerance to be closer to her. I knew Mrs. Felds was no doctor. It didn't matter. Even a nursing student was better than nothing, and I'd told her that the last time we met. I didn't want to have this baby alone. And, if I kept having to run for my life, I was afraid this baby wouldn't stay where it was supposed to.

As if the little freeloader knew I was thinking about it, it kicked hard. I winced and wished I had something to eat. Food always made the baby happy. It made me happy, too.

"It's about time," the man next to me murmured under his breath.

A moment later, someone touched my leg.

"Are you hurt?" Mrs. Felds asked.

I lifted my head and took another unsteady drink of juice to calm down the mini ninja trying to kick its way out of my stomach.

"I think I'm fine. My heart's just racing, and I can't stop shaking. But, I think everything is staying where it's supposed to be," I said, hoping I was right.

She nodded.

"I haven't forgotten my promise. When I finish up here, I'll come find you."

We were leaving this coffin. Today.

I wanted to grin, but too many people were watching us closely, including the stern looking fey behind her. Not wanting to do anything to jeopardize my chance of leaving with her, I settled for a chill nod and set my head back on my knees.

Mrs. Felds and her fey friend started asking the people waiting for her help where they were injured. While she took the first patient behind a screen, I gingerly got to my feet and shuffled to the bathroom.

It wasn't a long while before Matt's voice rang out with an all clear. But he warned those who wanted to leave the hangar that they should go out heavily armed.

"The fey have checked the grounds, but we all know the

infected are getting smarter. Don't take any chances. Go out, get what you need to live, and come back here."

"Here? For how long?" someone called out.

"Until it's safe," Matt said.

I snorted softly. Was it ever really safe?

I stayed where I was, leaning against the wall. There wasn't anything I needed badly enough from my tent to risk my life.

SHIFTING my weight from one foot to the other, I waited in line for the meager rations a few others had helped Bertha carry over from the cafeteria.

"Angel," Mrs. Felds called.

I looked toward the door, and she waved me over. I didn't want to leave my place in line, but the fey beside Mrs. Felds was helping her with her jacket. The chance to leave outweighed the need to eat.

I hurried over. Excitement and fear made my heart race again. Leaving Whiteman meant leaving the protection of the fence. It also meant being touched, something I'd avoided since the earthquakes.

"We're going?" I asked softly when I reached them.

"Yes. Do you need to grab anything from your tent?" Mrs. Felds asked.

I shook my head.

"No clothes?"

"It's no big deal, Mrs. Felds," I said, not wanting to talk about it. "I'm ready to go whenever you are."

The truth was that nothing in that tent fit me anymore. The leggings under my unbuttoned, loose jeans kept me warm, and the shirts I wore tucked into the waistband of the jeans helped keep my pants up. It worked.

"Okay. But call me Cassie," she said with a kind smile.

Kerr, Cassie's fey companion, led the way out the door. The people in the hangar didn't even notice us leaving. Or if they did, they didn't make a big deal out of it.

The wind stole my breath for a moment as I stepped outside. A few flakes drifted down from the cloudy sky. I hated snow. Shivering at the temperature change, I pulled up the hood of my jacket and took the mittens from my pocket. I could never seem to get warm enough anymore.

"Brog," Kerr called to a fey jogging past.

The large man changed direction and stopped before us.

"How many females did they lose?" Brog asked.

"Five."

Both of the men looked truly upset by the news.

"Twelve people total," Cassie said. "I hope Matt takes my suggestion seriously. This base is too big to defend with the people they have."

"We could send more fey," Kerr said.

"Which is fine for a short-term solution. Long term, this is just too much area to defend."

Kerr grunted. I wasn't sure if it was acknowledgment or disagreement, though.

"Brog, we need to return to Tolerance. Will you carry Angel?"

Brog looked at me and nodded. I'd known this was coming. There was only one safe way to get anywhere, and it wasn't in a loud infected-attracting vehicle. It was in the arms of a fey. I'd seen numerous girls get a lift that way. Honestly, it looked pretty awesome. If I knew the fey wouldn't catch on to my baby bump, I'd try to hitch a ride like that everywhere. However, they were a little handsy when they carried their prizes.

Brog stepped toward me.

"May I carry you, Angel?"

"Yes. Thank you." He lifted me gently and settled me against his torso. I kept my arm wedged between him and my stomach to help prevent Brog from feeling any tiny ninja kicks.

"It's colder when the fey run," Cassie said. "Turn your face toward Brog, or it'll rob you of breath."

I didn't need to be told twice. I set my face against his warmth.

"Brog, warn Angel before you jump the wall. It might upset her stomach."

Wall? That sounded intimidating and promising all at the same time.

"I will," Brog said.

A moment later, he was moving. The chill seeped through my clothes before we even reached the gate. Brog tried to hold me a little closer as we left Whiteman, but my elbow prevented too much cuddling.

I shivered before too long but didn't complain. Noise outside of the fence was a death sentence. Even as the fey ran, I could hear the infected call to each other.

"We're almost there," Brog said quietly.

I nodded and kept quiet.

"Here's the wall."

That was the only warning I had before he jumped. My stomach wasn't even done somersaulting when he landed on the other side half a second later.

I lifted my head and got my first look at the place I would now call home. The country neighborhood had been converted into an extremist gated community, using vehicles that stood on their ends and were wedged together to form a solid wall. The heavy-duty barrier cut through the trees, some having been removed to create a clear path along the inside of the wall. Based on my view and the lack of the tree branches I could see on the other side, I guessed the fey had done the same outside as well.

"It's okay," Cassie said. "I'll take Angel from here."

Brog reluctantly set me on my feet as I noted the backs of houses in front of us. Between them, I saw more houses. There weren't any infected anywhere.

"Thanks for carrying me, Brog," I said when I realized he was staring at me.

"I will be back in two days, my Angel."

"Oh, whoa. I'm not your Angel. I'm not anyone's anything."

Cassie stepped up beside me.

"Brog, you know that's not how this works. Just because

you're interested in her doesn't mean she's interested in you. And what about Dawnn? I thought you were trying to charm her."

The fey's yellow eyes darted to Cassie.

"She told me to go away and never come back."

Cassie smiled at him. "And you're going to listen?"

He grunted.

"You'd better head back to Whiteman. Matt needs all the help he can get."

Brog gave me one last contemplative look then jumped over the wall.

Cassie faced Kerr.

"I'll show Angel where she's going to stay and meet you at home when I'm done."

He grabbed her and kissed her hard. Obviously, she wasn't Mrs. Felds anymore.

It no longer seemed weird to see the grey-skinned behemoths around. I'd grown used to their pointed ears and lizard-like eyes. However, this level of intensity was new for me. I'd seen them pine for women but hadn't ever been up close when one scored a kiss. And holy hell was it enough to make me blush.

When he pulled away, I averted my gaze. It wasn't that I was a prude; I was just jealous as shit. No one had ever looked at me with the complete adoration Kerr was using on Cassie just now. Not even the guy who'd knocked me up. Which was okay with me. He'd been a fun fling but too high most of the time to count on. It was safer just to count on myself.

"Don't take too long," Kerr said huskily.

Cassie cleared her throat, drawing my attention as Kerr walked away.

"Displays of affection are definitely their thing," she said. "Public or private. Doesn't seem to matter to them."

"It's okay. It didn't bother me."

She started out in the same direction Kerr had gone. We moved at a much slower pace, though.

"So, officially welcome to Tolerance." She gestured to all the houses. "It's going to feel weird at first. Living in a house. Showering. Wearing actual pajamas to bed instead of ready-to-run layers. But you really can do all of that without any fear. The infected never try to come in here."

An infected called out distantly, and she frowned a little.

"Before this morning, the infected didn't even come close."

"What changed?" I asked.

"I'm not sure. But it doesn't change the fact that they won't get in." She pointed up toward the walls, and I spotted the fey walking along the tops of the cars. Movement near the base caught my eye. A fey watched us and waved when he saw I'd spotted him. I averted my gaze and saw another fey.

"They're all over the place," I said softly.

"Does that bother you?"

"Hell no. I'm sleeping in my damn underwear tonight."

She chuckled, getting what I meant. With all these fey, I knew I'd be safe from the infected.

"What about the hellhounds?" I asked.

"Watch," she said. Almost as if on cue, twin beams of light shot up into the sky from one of the cars.

"Wow."

"Yep. The lights stay on all night. Keeps the hounds out. Any that get close, the fey go after. Either way, there's no hounds getting in here."

"The batteries don't die?"

"No. The fey and Mya's dad hooked them up to a solar charged battery bank. All the houses here have been converted to solar, too."

"I get why you think Whiteman needs to go to something like this. It's perfect."

"It has its quirks like any other place. But it's safe. That's what counts."

She stopped in front of a house and flipped the flag on the mailbox down.

"This place is yours," she said. "There are supplies in the storage shed for the ba—"

I grabbed her arm and looked at her with wide eyes, unable to believe what she'd been about to blurt. A fey crossed the street a few yards away, nodded at us, and cut between the yards.

"Please. Don't talk about it," I begged quietly. "I don't want anyone to know."

"It's going to be hard to keep it a secret for very long," she said. Her gaze held pity and understanding.

"I know. But I'd like your promise you won't say anything until I'm ready."

"I'll stay quiet unless my silence jeopardizes your health.

And you should know, once one fey knows something, they'll all know it. They information-share like crazy."

"Good to know." I released my hold on her, relieved she wouldn't say anything.

"I live four houses down." She said the house number. "If you need anything, just let me know."

I nodded and stood on the street, staring at the house as she walked away. I couldn't believe I got a whole house. Relief and excitement bubbled through me.

"There's nowhere to go but up," I said softly, resisting the urge to pat my belly.

CHAPTER TWO

My stomach gurgled noisily, the sound echoing in the shower over the sound of the water.

"I know, I know." I patted my belly with one hand as I turned in the spray to rinse my hair.

The fact that I hadn't found a speck of food in the house last night had depressed me a little. But, I understood that food was growing scarcer with the infected making supply runs more difficult. Instead of focusing on what I couldn't have, I chose to focus on what I could. Last night, I'd slept in my underwear under a thick quilt while the furnace blew warm air throughout the house. This morning, I was leisurely showering for the first time in weeks without the fear of discovery.

I turned in the water again, loving the heat and the scent of soap. I'd even found a razor to shave my pits and legs.

"Heaven," I said to myself. "This right here is a piece of it."

With a wistful sigh, I turned off the water and dried off. My clothes waited on the counter. I dressed and then basked in the feel of soft, clean clothes, thanks to the washer, dryer, and privacy I now had access to.

"This is the life, little biscuit. All we need is some food to make it perfect."

My wet hair hung down my back after I brushed it out. The crazy length is why I normally kept it braided. Plus, the braid helped to keep my hair cleaner, which meant less showering and possible risk of exposure. Now, none of that really mattered.

Smiling, I went downstairs and looked around the kitchen. After I'd thoroughly searched it last night and had come up with nothing, I'd been too tired to search anywhere else. My gaze drifted to the basement door, and I exhaled heavily.

I hated basements. They were creepy before the infected and hellhounds started hiding in the dark. Now, they had the potential to be terrifyingly deadly.

"But people like putting homemade stuff in their basements. And, we like pickles now, don't we, ninja?"

I shuffled closer, really not wanting to do what I knew I needed to do. Story of my life. And, just like every other time I was faced with a difficult situation, I got inventive. Humming a few notes for Twinkle, Twinkle, I start singing new lyrics to the old melody as I approached the door.

"Step by step I'll walk downstairs, acting like I have no cares. In the dark so cold and still, an infected waits for the kill. Bite by bite I'd terribly die, and no one here will even cry."

I reached for the doorknob. Just before my hand closed over it, someone knocked. I jumped, my mouth opening for a scream when I realized the knock came from behind me, not in front.

Releasing a shaky exhale, I quickly put on the two shirts I had waiting on the kitchen chair. Feeling confident that I looked fat and not pregnant, I opened the door.

A young woman stood on the stoop. Warmly dressed, with her light brown hair tucked into the hood of her winter jacket, she smiled at me. She looked close to my age, which didn't surprise me. The young and fit survived well.

She lifted a plate with a large slice of cake on it.

"Hi, my name's Emily. Welcome to the neighborhood."

"Thanks. I'm Angel. Would you like to come in?"

I stepped back and motioned her in, my eyes never leaving the cake.

She laughed and stepped inside.

"I figured cake would help win you over."

That got my attention.

"Is there a reason I need to be won over?" I asked as I accepted the plate.

"Word is that you just want to be left alone. According to Cassie, anyway."

"Ah. I do, but I'll always welcome cake." I pinched off a piece and ate it. My stomach immediately demanded more, and I tried to look unhurried as I turned to search for a fork.

"I was hoping you'd be willing to come over to my place

for a very small party. I love living here. It's safe. But it's also boring as hell."

Whiteman had been boring, too, until the infected found the next, new way in. Boring was safe. Excitement never meant something good. But I didn't say that. Instead, I plucked a fork out of the drawer and took a bigger bite. The cake was okay. I wasn't really a dessert person, but any food was much appreciated these days. And parties usually meant more food.

"All right," I said. "What time should I be there?"

She beamed at me.

"How about just after noon?"

"Works for me." I took another bite of cake and chewed happily as she told me her house number then waved and let herself out.

As soon as I licked the plate clean, I went to the living room where I'd found a stack of PG movies. I picked a cartoon and turned on the TV, willing to forgo any basement exploration now that my belly was happier.

The clock slowly ticked away the minutes. The moment it said it was noon, I finished getting ready and walked out the door. The brisk air chilled my cheeks as I looked at the numbers of the homes around me. It was easy to spot which direction to go. And easier still to identify Emily's house, even without seeing the house number. The front door stood partially open, and the soft thump of music echoed from within.

I walked up the front step and saw Emily, another girl, and three fey already inside. The fey were the standard long-haired, well-muscled hotties variety that made me wish I was available for a night between the sheets. The girl I hadn't yet met had a head of dirty-blonde curls and laughter that held the attention of every fey in the room.

Emily spotted me before I reached the door.

"Angel. Right on time."

I stepped inside and reluctantly parted with my coat when she asked to take it. While she closed the door and hung my jacket, I looked at the table set up in the living room.

A stack of wine boxes sat on the surface, along with six crystal glasses. My gaze swept the rest of the open concept living room and kitchen. There wasn't a speck of food in sight.

"Angel, this is Hannah," Emily said, motioning to the girl with the curls. "And these guys are Shax, Tor, and Gyrik."

"Hi," I said with a polite smile.

Gyrik, the closest fey to me, moved even closer.

"Hello, Angel. Can I see you naked?"

Hannah and Emily smothered their laughter as Gyrik looked at me with a hopeful expression. He really was adorable with his earnestness. I hadn't met one of these grey devils that I hadn't liked yet.

"Sorry, big guy, but my naked days are on hold until the apocalypse is over."

He grunted and considered me for a moment.

"That may take a long time."

"A few years at least," I agreed.

He grunted, his expression hinting at his disappointment, and I felt bad for him. I wasn't a body-shy kind of person. If not for my belly, I would have totally taken him to a bedroom and let him look his fill. I'd heard that's all they wanted—just a glimpse of the female form—because they didn't have any female versions of their kind.

"I'm sure you'll find someone willing to take a walk on the wild side with you. Hang in there." I patted his arm and focused on the girls.

"So, what do you have to eat?" I asked with false cheer.

"Oh." Emily's face fell a little. "We didn't make anything. But…we have wine." She said the last bit like it was the most exciting thing in the world. A fucking bag of chips would have been the most exciting thing right then.

"I don't drink alcohol. It's against my religion," I lied with ease. "Is there any cake left?"

"I gave the rest to Mya to distract her. She's a party pooper."

"That does not mean she poops at parties," Gyrik said to me. "It means she does not like them."

"Ah. Thanks for the clarification. Do you have anything else to drink besides wine?" I asked Emily.

"Sorry. Just water."

Double strike.

"I'll have a glass of water, then." I smiled politely while inwardly cursing them.

While Hannah poured everyone else wine, Emily got my water.

"Do you play cards?" Hannah asked me.

"A bit. Mostly kids' games like go-fish."

"Perfect. Let's play that."

Since there wasn't any food, I wanted to leave. Yet, I sat at the table and agreed to play cards so they wouldn't know that I'd only come for the food. I couldn't afford to raise any suspicions about how truly self-motivated I was.

"What's everyone going to bet?" Hannah asked, dealing cards.

"I'll bet a kiss," Emily said. "No tongue."

"I'll bet a home-cooked meal," Hannah said.

"You should bet a kiss, too," Shax said to Hannah, looking serious.

"Nah. I'm not in the mood to kiss anyone."

"Not even me?" he asked.

"Anyone means everyone," she said. It wasn't unkind, yet I couldn't help feeling bad for the guy. He clearly had a thing for her.

"What about a hug?" he asked.

"No, Shax. Dinner. That's it."

He exhaled, clearly annoyed, and picked up his cards.

"I will bet a bag of sour cream and onion chips."

I'd been trying to figure out a way to back out, but his bet changed everything. Mama wanted chips.

"I will bet a hairbrush," Tor said.

"I will bet a candy bar," Gyrik said.

All eyes landed on me.

"I just got here and don't own a thing."

"Just bet walking you home. The guys'll be happy," Emily said.

"And if you two win?"

"Then we'll walk you home," Hannah said before

downing half her glass of wine like it was lemonade on a hot day.

The fey played with a shrewd deliberation that would have better fit a high stakes poker game than a game of Go Fish. The intelligent way they studied us when they asked for a card told me just how seriously they took this game. The girls were more relaxed. While they waited for their turn, they asked questions about life outside of Tolerance, Whiteman, and anything that the fey found interesting during their supply runs.

It surprised me to hear that Matt and a few fey had left Whiteman to scout possible new locations similar to Tolerance. It also made me twice as grateful that I had left the survivor camp when I had.

We played the first game for almost an hour before naming Shax the winner. The need to pee had me quickly getting up from the table and asking for the bathroom. Hannah walked with me down the hall.

"It sucks he won again," Hannah said before we reached the bathroom.

"Again?"

"The fey always win. Shax more than the rest. That's why I don't bet kisses anymore."

"Ah." I really didn't care about her reasons but felt it would have been rude not to say something before closing the door on her.

When I finished, she wasn't in the hallway, and I made my way back to the living room. Everyone was sitting at the table while Hannah dealt out another hand.

"This was a nice break from the monotony of fearing for my life, but I think I should head back to my house. I see a nap in my future because one good night's sleep didn't make up for all the crappy ones before it."

"Aw, are you sure?" Emily asked, standing to walk me to the front door.

"Yeah. Thanks for having me over, though."

"Shax," Hannah said. "Don't forget to collect your winnings."

"I want to spend more time with you," he said.

Emily quietly rolled her eyes and handed me my jacket.

"It's okay if you'd rather not walk with me," I said. "Sorry I didn't have anything better to bet."

"I will walk her home," Tor said, standing.

"Nope," Hannah said. "You know this isn't how it works. No trading off what you won. Shax, you're going to hurt Angel's feelings."

"Nope. He's really not." I tugged my jacket on and let myself out.

"Be sure to claim your kiss from Emily, too," Hannah called before the door closed behind me.

I shook my head.

"Weird people."

"Not weird," Shax said, making me scream and almost slip on the shoveled walkway. He caught my elbow to steady me.

"Holy crap, where did you come from?"

"The house."

"No kidding." He released me, and I took a few calming

breaths as I stepped away. "I was serious about you not needing to walk with me. It wouldn't have hurt my feelings. It's obvious you're into Hannah."

He grunted.

I'd noticed a long time ago that grunts in lieu of answers seemed to be a thing with the fey. It didn't bother me like it seemed to bug some of the other survivors. Especially Bertha. She hated their non-committal responses.

Thinking of her made me think of food, and my stomach growled. Damn it.

"Did you get your kiss from Emily?" I asked to distract myself.

"I do not want Emily's kisses."

He sounded frustrated and angry. I didn't take it personally.

"Just Hannah's kisses, huh?"

"Yes. I do not understand why she will not give me more of them like she does with her hugs when I bring her things."

It didn't take a genius to figure out Hannah's real game.

"Oh? What kinds of things earn you hugs?"

"She hugged me for the wine. I liked the way her breasts pressed against me." He rubbed his stomach, which was probably where her breasts had touched given his height.

"A hug for all that wine? I'd kiss you with my tongue if you showed up with a pizza." Hell, I'd do a lot more than that for a pizza. I went a little tingly at the thought of sex. It's been way too long since I'd enjoyed that.

"I will not cheat on Hannah," Shax said seriously, interrupting my nostalgic thoughts.

I studied him for a moment while we walked. An idea slowly formed. Hannah was obviously using the fey for information and any supplies she could talk out of them. I couldn't fault her for what she was doing. Sure, I felt bad for the guys, but I understood her motivation. She'd found a way to survive. I had to be smart like that, too.

The bottom line was that I needed food. I placed my hand on my stomach for a brief moment. However, unlike with Hannah, I'd be fair with Shax. I'd make sure the benefits weren't so one-sided. Both parties needed to get what they wanted.

"I think we can help each other, Shax."

"What do you mean?"

"You're having a hard time winning over Hannah, right?"

"Yes."

"Well, I'm hungry all the time. How about I help you learn what girls really want, and you help me by bringing me some extra food when you can."

"You will tell me what Hannah wants for her kisses?"

"No, because you don't want just Hannah's kisses. You need to think bigger."

"Her breasts?"

These guys really did have a physical focus.

"Her affection. If you have her heart, then kisses, boobs, and all the rest will be yours too. To do that, I will tell you what Hannah wants in a man."

"Yes. That is what I want. All of her. I want to taste her pussy. Kerr said it's better than food."

My mind went blank for a moment. Big, caring, and a

craving to go down on a girl? Damn it! Why was I always drawing the short straw in life?

"Er...Okay. It's good to have goals. But if we're going to do this, you can't tell anyone," I said, recalling Cassie's comment about the fey being gossips. "If I find out you're telling your friends what I'm telling you or that I'm helping you, then the deal' s off."

"I understand."

"Not even a hint," I pressed. The last thing I needed was a whole bunch of the fey knocking on my door and drawing more unwanted attention to me. I was safe enough with Shax because of the love goggles he wore for Hannah.

"I will say nothing. Not even a hint."

"Okay. Then, the first thing you need to know is that you have to stop seeming so desperate. It turns girls off."

"But I am desperate. I can think of nothing else but Hannah. I would do anything for her."

"I think that's part of the problem."

"What do you mean?"

"Well, at the party the girls mentioned that Mya wouldn't like that they had the wine. And, you're the one who brought the wine. I'm taking a guess here, but it would be you who got in trouble if Mya found out that you provided the wine, right?"

He grunted.

"Women don't like men who are lapdogs."

"I am not a dog."

I laughed lightly.

"It's a saying. Not something literal. You're not a dog, but you're acting docile like one. Women don't want docile. Not out of a sexy grey devil like you. I've seen what you can do. You're strong. You're intense. And that's great. That's what women need in this world if they want to survive. You have to show Hannah that. And if she asks you to do something that you know is wrong, you have to stand up for yourself and say no. If she's a good person, she'll understand. If she doesn't understand, you need to ask yourself if you really want to be with a person who is okay with getting you into trouble."

We reached my house, and he walked me up to the door.

"I'm glad that I walked you home, Angel. Thank you."

"No problem."

Before I could ask if he happened to have those chips on him, he nodded and took off at a run.

"Damn," I said under my breath.

My stomach growled in agreement.

CHAPTER THREE

I LET MYSELF INSIDE THE HOUSE AND SIGHED IN RELIEF THAT I was alone again. Going to Emily's sad excuse for a party hadn't been a completely useless risk. Hopefully, the deal with Shax would pay off. Sure, it sucked that he took off before I could shake him down for something to eat, but the fey kept their word. I knew he'd show up again with something for me.

Besides, my deal with Shax was my plan B. Plan A was Cassie. When I'd first told her that I wanted to move with her to Tolerance, she'd been the one to talk to Matt about having Bertha serve me more food. Not that it had really worked. I hadn't wanted Bertha to know the real reason I needed more calories. But, that wasn't the point. The point was that my lack of food now had to be an oversight. All I needed to do was talk to Cassie about it.

I checked the window by the door and seeing the sidewalk clear, eagerly left the house again. However, no one answered the door four houses down even though I knocked several times.

Maybe she'd put her kids down for a nap. It wasn't like there was a ton to do with young kids anymore. Tolerance didn't have any parks or zoos, and I couldn't see her removing the kids from Tolerance's protective wall for trivial reasons.

Not wanting to draw attention to myself, I went home again.

Hungry and irritated, I hung up my jacket and kicked off my shoes before going to the living room and flopping on the couch. The blanket I'd found in the closet the night before waited for me. Snuggling in, I turned on another movie. I liked the collection of shows. Cartoons were my thing. Too bad I didn't have any popcorn to go with them. I tried not to let myself feel too bitter about that.

My excuse of needing a nap was truer than I thought because my eyes closed after only a few minutes.

"She is a good person."

The loud, excited sound of Shax's voice and the bang of the door jolted me awake. I looked up and saw him walking in. He closed the kitchen door behind him and looked my way.

"What?" I asked, unsure what was going on.

He smiled widely, showing his sharp canines as he removed his jacket and hung it on the kitchen chair.

"Hannah is a good person," he said again. "I told her I did not want Mya angry with me and wanted to return the wine. Hannah said she understood. She even gave me a hug."

He made himself comfortable on the chair next to the couch and leaned forward, studying me. I nonchalantly pulled the blanket over my stomach, bunching it to hide the tell-tale bulge.

"You are very smart, Angel."

If I were so smart, I wouldn't have been so damn hungry; but I kept that thought to myself.

"What do I do now?" he asked

"Now, you give her some space."

He groaned and sat back in his chair.

"I do not like space."

I chuckled softly.

"You might not like space, but she'll like it. Especially after you were acting so desperate."

"It was not acting. What I feel is real. I need her."

I shook my head at him.

"This is what I'm talking about. You've got to keep that shit in. No girl wants to hear how desperate you are for her."

He scowled at me.

"Why?"

"Would you want to hear how desperate a girl is for you? Would you want her there begging for your attention every time you turn around?"

"Yes."

"Okay." I got up and plopped myself down in Shax's lap.

"I'm desperate for a real man, Shax. I want you to touch me. To taste my pussy."

He stood up and set me on my feet like I was on fire. It was almost laughable.

"I only want Hannah," he said firmly.

"I only want you, Shax. I can't think of anything else. Can I see you naked?"

His expression changed to one of complete shock, and I couldn't contain myself. I laughed so hard I almost peed.

"I do not understand your laughter," he said, crossing his arms.

I wiped at my eyes and sat down on the couch, using the blanket as a shield once more.

"Sit. I won't jump into your lap again. I promise. I did it to teach you something."

He frowned and slowly resumed sitting. I could see he was trying to figure out what the point of all that had been.

"I was Shax, and you were Hannah just now. I was telling you how desperate I was to see you naked, to touch you, and have you touch me. How did that make you feel?"

He grunted in response.

"How you felt might be similar to how Hannah feels every time you act like that around her."

"I do not sit on her lap and ask her to taste my penis."

I had to look away for a moment so I wouldn't bust out laughing again. The struggle was real.

"I may have gone a bit extreme to prove my point," I said when I was in control. "I'm sorry if what I did upset you or hurt you in any way."

He exhaled slowly.

"You did not hurt me. Thank you for helping me understand what Hannah is feeling."

"Not what she is feeling. What she might be feeling. You

need to ask yourself how you would feel if the roles were reversed. And not just with Hannah but with anyone else. It'll help you get an idea what another person is feeling."

"I understand."

He looked completely depressed, though.

"Come on, big guy. Don't be down. Do you want to watch a movie with me? I'll teach you how to give a girl a foot rub that will have her—" I stopped myself from saying that her panties would be dropping within twenty minutes.

"Will have her what?"

"Thinking that you might not be desperate. Just a really good man."

"Yes. I want to learn to rub feet."

Within five minutes, the movie was playing, and I was getting the best foot rub of my life. Any time I started feeling a little guilty about it, I reminded myself that my lessons would make some woman extremely happy in the future. And, Shax seemed pretty content with his task now that he understood I wasn't going to molest him.

"Are fish always this forgetful?" he asked as he watched the TV.

I grinned.

"Nah, this isn't real. Just pretend stuff. But it has some good lessons. Like helping each other out."

He grunted and rubbed circles into the arch of my foot. Unable to help myself, I groaned and closed my eyes. He stopped.

"Groaning is good," I said. "Don't stop when you're doing something that makes a girl groan."

He started rubbing again.

"And, once a girl groans with you just rubbing her feet, you can take that as a sign to work your way a little further up her leg. Let's say, mid-calf. If you get another groan, go to the knee. If you get another groan after that, you can work your way up further."

His rubbing slowed.

"A foot rub can lead to tasting Hannah's pussy?"

"Only if she keeps groaning and does not tell you to stop." I opened one eye to peer at him. He wore a kid-in-the-candy-store look, and I knew he hadn't really heard that last part.

"Shax," I said, poking him in the ribs with my big toe. "You need to listen to this part."

"Yes. Only if she keeps groaning. Stop means stop."

"Okay." I set my foot back in his lap. My heel brushed something really long and really hard.

"What else can lead to tasting Hannah's pussy?" he asked.

"Eh…I think one hint at a time is enough. Remember, you don't want to seem desperate. And if you go from trying a foot rub to trying something else, that will definitely look desperate to her."

He growled softly.

"There are too many rules."

I grinned.

"Girls are complicated. The right girls are worth the effort, though."

He set my feet aside and stood.

"I must go," he said.

"Okay. Thanks for hanging out with me."

He grabbed his jacket and practically ran out the door.

"I sure hope he doesn't show up on Hannah's doorstep with that boner and an offer to rub her feet," I said to myself as I focused on the movie.

I BASKED in my own cleanliness. A shower two mornings in a row was pure bliss. Almost as blissful as eating the bag of chips I'd discovered on the kitchen table after Shax had left the night before.

Brushing out my hair, I studied my naked reflection. I was too thin. I had sticks for arms and legs, which made my belly seem even bigger by comparison. I didn't know how Shax hadn't noticed last night. It had to be his complete fixation on Hannah that kept him blind to what was going on with me. And that worked in my benefit big time.

Hungry, I dressed and went downstairs. Eating all the chips last night left nothing for breakfast. That meant I couldn't avoid the basement any longer.

I flicked on the switch and carefully went down the steps, my grip tight around the baseball bat I'd found in the front closet. The bat wasn't for infected; it was for spiders. They were the only creature which I stood a chance of defending myself against in this pit of despair I was entering.

The stairs ended near a wall, like too many basements tended to do. Light from the stairwell extended a few feet to the right and left, my two options. I didn't see a switch in either direction.

Humming to myself, I peeked around the right. Boxes were stacked in a disarrayed pile and cobwebs hung from the ceiling. I exhaled slowly and looked to the left. That space was devoid of anything but the furnace and water heater.

I shuffled to the right and prayed a spider wouldn't drop onto my head.

The boxes contained family pictures and personal items like trophies and awards. I slowly resealed the cardboard flaps, understanding that someone had carefully packed the previous family's things away. Maybe the people who'd lived here would be back someday and want the memories. But, most likely, those people were already dead.

Taking my bat, I explored further into that half of the poorly lit space and found an empty tank near a storage rack that had long lights hung from the bottom of each shelf. I stepped closer and looked at the dead, wilted plants in the pots of dirt. A sense of excitement filled me. It wasn't the canned goods I was hoping for, but it was a potential food source.

As I reached out for the pull string to test one of the lights, I slid my foot forward. My toe bumped something just under the bottom shelf. A second later, something darted out. Long and fast, the body slithered between my feet.

I screamed, threw the bat at it, and ran the other direction. The bat hit the floor with a clank then bounced and hit me behind the knee, taking me down like a bullet to the back. As I fell, I could only think "not the floor. The snake is on the floor."

My screaming never stopped as I caught myself on my hands and knees and scrambled to my feet. Wild-eyed, I grabbed the bat. With a two-handed grip, I ended the snake's existence, caveman style, while it was trying to find a place to hide in the box pile.

"I'm a fucking amazon!" I yelled at the gory lump, my heart thundering in my chest.

Something thundered down the steps, and I laughed like a crazy woman when I saw Shax's face.

"I heard you scream," he said. "Why are you laughing now?"

"I just beat the shit out of a snake." I pointed, shaking uncontrollably.

He glanced at the snake as he came toward me.

"And that is funny?"

"No. It's terrifying."

I grabbed his hand and placed his fingers on my throat, right above my pulse.

"Feel that? My heart is jacked. Can I get a ride upstairs to the couch? I think I need to sit down for a minute."

He scooped me in his arms without hesitation and carried me upstairs. While I continued to shake, I asked for a glass of water. It took several minutes to calm down after that. Shax sat in his chair and quietly watched me.

"What brings you back?" I asked when I could think rationally again.

"I saw Hannah. I was not desperate, but she would not let me rub her feet. She told me to go away."

While I was clubbing snakes in my basement, he was desperately trying to get his snake in someone's downstairs. I fought not to grin.

"Why are you so into Hannah? What's so great about her?"

His expression grew distant and a bit wistful. The crotch of his pants twitched a little, and I knew he'd found his happy place.

"She let me touch her breast."

The reverent way he said the words worried me. I waited for him to say more, but he didn't.

"That's it? You're hot for Hannah because you felt her up one time?"

I stood and grabbed his hands. Before he could guess my intent, I placed his palms over my boobs. He tried to pull away, but I kept my hands over his.

"They're just boobs, Shax. Something that all women have in varying degrees. Give them a squeeze." I moved his hands over my breasts and watched him frown. "Big or small or none at all…feeling someone's breasts isn't the basis for the devotion you're showing Hannah."

"I understand." He paused for a moment, and I felt his fingers lightly squeeze over me. It sent a tingle in all the right places before he pulled his hands away and rubbed them on his legs with a guilty look on his face.

"I know you are trying to teach me something, but I do not like cheating on Hannah."

"Shax, you're not cheating. Do you know why?"

He frowned and shook his head.

"Because you and Hannah aren't together yet. Until she says she wants to be with you, she's not yours. Do you understand?"

The guilty look melted to one of frustration.

"But she is mine."

"Okay. If Hannah's yours, you must know a lot about her. Tell me what she likes."

I resumed my seat on the couch.

"She likes wine."

"I knew that the first time I saw her gulp half a glass. Does that mean she's mine, too?"

He scowled.

"I'll take that as a no. I'm not trying to burst your bubble here, Shax; I'm trying to help you understand Hannah. Now, do you think Hannah likes you?"

"Yes. She likes when I bring her things."

"Of course she does. Any girl would. I liked it when I found the chips on the table last night. Does that mean I like you the way you want Hannah to like you?"

"No."

"You're right. No, it doesn't. All you really know about Hannah is that she likes things. Her desire for those things is the reason she invites you to her parties for her games and betting. It has nothing to do with her interest in you."

He tensed in his chair. The anger that clouded his expression was truly formidable.

"Hannah does not just like me for the things I bring her," he said.

"Okay," I said, holding up my hands in surrender. "No peeing on the Hannah altar. Got it."

He paused for a moment, and I knew he wasn't sure what I meant.

"I bring you things." His tone held accusation.

"You're right. You have brought me things. But what we have going on is a deal. A fair trade we both agreed to up front. I'm getting something in return for giving you something of equal value. Well, it's supposed to be equal value. You're getting the better end of this deal for sure. You can't say the same with all the deals you've had with Hannah. Six boxes of wine for a hug is crazy unfair."

His tension melted away, and he slumped into his chair.

"She did not give me a hug," he said reluctantly. "She said thank you."

"Oh, hun. That's just sad," I said, feeling truly sorry for him. "You need to spend some quality time with Hannah to get to know her. Find out what she likes versus what you like. You might be surprised to learn she's not thinking about sex all the time like you are."

"I do not think about sex all the time."

"Let me guess, you think about tasting pussy and breasts, too."

"Yes."

I grinned and said nothing.

He grunted, and his gaze dropped to the floor. That was one thing about these fey. They were naïve about a lot, but they weren't stupid. They caught on eventually. I tugged the blanket up over my stomach, feeling a smidge of concern even though I was dressed in baggy layers for the day.

"What is quality time?" he asked, interrupting my thoughts.

"It's where you just spend time together. Talk. Maybe watch a movie or have dinner."

He stood and looked at me.

"Thank you, Angel."

"Any time, Shax. Deal or not, I'm going to do what I can to help you win over Hannah. But I wouldn't mind another bag of chips."

"Mya said that Bertha needs smaller portions. That's why her belly is so big. I will try to find you a small bag of chips." He glanced meaningfully at my belly.

My mouth dropped open, and I scrambled to my feet.

"You think I'm fat?"

He shrugged, and I laughed, unable to help myself.

"You laugh at odd things," he said.

"You have no idea."

I walked him to the door.

"Can I give you a hug, Shax," I asked after he put his jacket on.

"Why?"

"I want to give you something with no strings attached. No conditions. No trades. Just me giving you a hug, so you know what a free hug feels like. How they're supposed to be given."

He nodded.

Given all the layers between us and his new belief I was fat, I wrapped my arms around him and hugged him hard.

"Thanks for being you, Shax," I said against his sleeve. "Don't change. You're pretty awesome."

His arms came around me, and he gave a light squeeze.

"Thank you for being my friend."

I pulled back before I got emotional.

"Good luck with Hannah," I said, reaching for the door. "And please don't tell anyone about my snake handling skills earlier. I don't want anyone to think I can't—"

I pulled the door open and jumped at the sight of two surprised faces.

Cassie looked from me to Shax then back to me.

"You've been handling Shax's snake?" Cassie asked.

CHAPTER FOUR

THE DARK-HAIRED WOMAN HELD OUT HER HAND, AMUSEMENT lighting her gaze.

"I'm Mya," she said as we shook. "Never thought anyone would distract you from Hannah, Shax. I'm so happy you finally found someone."

I wanted to die a little on the inside that they thought I'd been referring to Shax's "snake." Did they really think I was messing around with one of the fey my second day here? That wasn't a good first impression, even if it was technically true.

Shax frowned as he glanced at me.

"You're going to give him a mental breakdown," I said to Cassie and Mya. "Shax, you should go. And good luck. Cassie, Mya, please come in."

Shax reluctantly stepped out, his brow slightly furrowed.

"Is Caden at your house?" he asked Cassie.

"He is. I'm sure he'd like to see you if you want to stop by."

He grunted and left. Cassie and Mya waited until the door closed before bombarding me with conversation.

"How did you get him to notice you?"

"I didn't think you were ready for that kind of attention."

"It does seem a bit fast."

"Are you sure——"

I held up my hands to stop the barrage.

"Shax is still interested in Hannah. I clubbed a snake to death in my basement and screamed like a madwoman. Shax heard and rushed in. I didn't want anyone to know about the snake because I don't want anyone thinking it's too dangerous for me to be here by myself. I love the safety and the isolation."

"Oh…" they both said at the same time.

The smell of cooked food drew my attention to Mya's hands and the small square baking pan she held.

"Can I take that for you?" I offered. My mouth was already watering with all of the possibilities I imagined hidden within the tinfoil-covered dish. It smelled like bacon. Maybe even eggs. Please let it be bacon and eggs, I thought.

"There was a snake in your basement?" Cassie shivered and glanced at the door which still stood open. "I am so glad I did not stay in this house."

"Are you okay?" Mya asked.

"I'm fine. Seriously, I can take that dish for you." I didn't wait for permission but took it right out of her hands.

"We can have breakfast together," I said as I headed

toward the kitchen counter. I hoped I sounded relaxed and not desperately in need of food. There was a rustle of noise behind me. When I turned, both women had removed their jackets and were already sitting at the table.

While I talked about the episode in the basement, I plated our portions, which I'd divided into three relatively equal sizes. I wasn't sure exactly what it was, but it looked like some kind of breakfast bake with bacon, eggs, and hash browns. Cheese strings clung to the serving spoon, so I knew that was in there as well. This meal was going to be heaven.

With effort, I focused on making conversation instead of drooling.

"I think the snake came from the tank I noticed down there. I'm hoping it was just the one snake living in it."

"You should have had Shax check," Mya said.

"Honestly, I was so freaked out I didn't even think of it. I don't even know how I killed the thing." I sat down and took the first bite.

"Oh my gosh. This is so good," I said around my mouthful of food.

Mya smiled.

"I'll tell my mom, Julie. She was up early this morning, baking." Mya glanced at Cassie. "She's going to have Savvy and Timmy over today. I guess Byllo and Jessie are going to go on a date."

"A date?" I asked. "Where is there to go for a date?"

"My guess would be the bedroom," Cassie said with a smirk.

Mya chuckled.

"That's probably what Byllo has in mind. I think he's going to make her dinner first, though, because he was asking Mom a lot of questions about cooking. I'm just excited that another fey has found a girl."

While they discussed whoever this Byllo and Jessie pair were, I tried to pace each bite I placed in my mouth. I also tried to chew more than five times before swallowing, but it was hard. I wanted the food in my belly now.

"I can't believe you guys actually have eggs, hash browns, and bacon here to make something like this," I said when there was a lull in conversation.

"Yeah. Mom can really cook with what the fey have been finding. Unfortunately, this is the last of it," Mya said. "At least until the guys can restock what we had to give to Whiteman this morning."

"Oh?" I said, feeling confused. Whiteman always received a portion of supplies after the fey went out on a supply run. However, my understanding was that Tolerance kept their fair share since they rounded up the supplies.

"We just got word this morning that some infected had gotten into the cafeteria during the last attack. They'd taken a lot of food, leaving trails of it outside the fence and into the woods. While the fey guarding Whiteman were able to clean out more infected and recover some of the food, they didn't find it all."

"Wow," I said.

Mya sighed and nodded.

"The infected are getting really smart about our supplies," Cassie said. "They're starting to set traps in grocery stores and are just waiting for hungry people to risk their life for something to eat."

I swallowed hard, feeling royally screwed. Why was it so difficult to safely obtain something to eat in this world? If the infected were going after the things that we needed, like food, what would be next?

I pushed my worry aside and focused on what I had. A really good meal for the first time in a long time.

"Well, I'm glad I got to sample some of your mom's cooking with the supplies that were left."

"I'll be sure to pass on your appreciation. This was the least I could do for you."

"What do you mean?" I asked.

I glanced at Cassie, wondering if she had already broken her promise and spilled my big secret.

"I heard about the party," Mya said. "Thank you for convincing Shax to return the wine."

"You know about that? That it was me?"

That big-mouthed brat was going to get an earful next time I saw him. He obviously didn't understand the concept of a secret. Our deal was officially off.

"I figured it out when Hannah mentioned you were at the party," Mya said. "No one else would have tried talking Shax into returning the wine. Certainly not Hannah or Emily."

"They invited me to a drinking party when I first got here, too," Cassie said. "They seem to like to drink a lot."

Mya shrugged. "I don't think it's the drinking that they're after as much as it is the forgetting."

"Why?" I asked.

"When the fey and I found Hannah and Emily's group, they were stuck in a dead RV surrounded by a horde of infected. It wasn't looking good for the group. I can't imagine what they were mentally going through while waiting for the infected to figure out how to get in."

I nodded and took my last bite of breakfast. It was a survivor story. We'd all gone through something terrible in order to live. That was just the way it was now.

I glanced at Mya's plate and realized she'd only taken a single bite. Cassie shook her head slightly when I looked at her almost empty plate.

Mya chuckled.

"It's okay, Cassie," Mya said. "If Angel doesn't know yet, she will know soon, anyway. That's just how things are here."

"What do you mean?" I asked.

"The fey like to talk."

"So I've heard."

"I'm sick," Mya said without preamble.

As soon as she said it, I could see it. The sallow tint of her cheeks, and the dark circles under her eyes. Like me, she looked a bit too thin. Her pupils were even a little dilated.

"I don't know why, but I seem to be turning into one of the fey after my time in their caves. My skin is turning grey in patches, and I'm immune to infected bites like they are."

"Holy shit," I breathed.

"I wouldn't mind being like one of them, except the change is hurting me. Headaches. Vomiting. A lot of general pain that's getting worse every day. I think it's because the change is happening faster for me, unlike the fey who had thousands of years to become what they are."

I wasn't sure what to say to that. The idea of being immune to the infected was amazing. What she was going through to be immune didn't sound as fun.

"It's okay," Mya said. "It is what it is. There's no use worrying over things we can't change when there's too much other shit we can."

"I couldn't agree more," I said, really liking her. I hoped whatever was making her sick would pass. I knew she was the reason the fey were here, helping us, and didn't want to consider what they would do if she wasn't here.

She pushed her plate toward me.

"I only took the one bite. If you cut off that corner, you can probably have the rest. I'm pretty sure what I have isn't contagious."

Contagious or not I would have done anything to eat the rest of her food. Instead of shoving the food into my watering mouth like I wanted, I just stood and went to the cupboards to get a container instead.

"I'll save it for later," I said. Later being the moment they walked out the door.

"So, about Shax," Mya said while I finished clearing the table. "Any chance you're interested in him?"

I grinned.

"That man is so hung up on Hannah it's not even funny."

Mya nodded. "It's too bad Hannah's not into him. I've tried so many different ways to get those two together, and nothing seems to stick."

Cassie shook her head.

"Maybe you should stop trying then," she said.

"That's why I asked Angel if she was interested."

Minus the apparent shortage of food, Tolerance was shaping up to be a pretty amazing place to live. Everyone got along, and there was no human-fey animosity. The matchmaking was more amusing than annoying.

"Life is complicated enough without adding a fey into the mix," I said to Mya.

"What? No way. They uncomplicate things. Think of how the snake thing would have gone down if you had a guy in your life. He could have killed it for you."

Cassie snorted.

"Right. And then he would have locked you in your room fearing a new threat to your general health and safety. You're right. Way uncomplicated."

Mya shrugged. "The perks balance the drawbacks." She suddenly frowned and looked at me.

"What were you doing in the basement anyway?"

"Exploring, out of boredom," I said smoothly. "Is there a duty roster I'm supposed to be checking?"

"Pft. The fey aren't really keen on women pulling their own weight."

"They'd rather carry it," Cassie said. "Literally if you let them."

"So what do they want us to do?" I asked.

"Be a princess in a tower," Mya said. "So they can rescue you and maybe win your heart."

"Okay. And what's option B?"

"Dance naked in the streets," Cassie said.

Mya nodded. "That would be their first option if you were willing."

"Yeah, I think I'll make up an option C."

"Smart choice," Mya said.

"Do you know if anyone has any seeds?" I asked.

"I think there's still some in the supply shed. Why?"

"I found some growing lamps and pots by the snake tank. If there's seeds, I can try growing something." Not only would it give me something to do, but it would also help fill my belly in future months.

"That's great," Mya said. "Establishing some fresh produce now would go a long way in a few months. Especially if the supply runs keep getting harder. Help yourself to what's there. I'll put the word out that the fey should look for some more lights."

Cassie and Mya stayed for a while, talking about Whiteman and Tolerance and all the survivors and fey. It was interesting to get a glimpse into their lives here at Tolerance. The more they talked about the hardships that both places were facing, though, the more I knew I couldn't ask for additional food in front of Mya. At least, not without having a damn good reason. So when they were ready to leave, I pasted a smile on my face and said nothing.

I would try to catch Cassie later.

MY STOMACH MADE a pathetic gurgling sound, a protest at

being empty after two meals of Julie's amazing breakfast casserole. It wanted more. Unfortunately, I didn't have anything else.

Sitting at the kitchen table, I tapped my fingers on the wooden surface and studied the cloudy sky through the window. The sun was only an hour from setting. Surely, Cassie would be home by now.

I got up from the table and put on my jacket. If I couldn't find Cassie at home, I'd walk around until I found her. I couldn't put off talking to her for another day.

When I opened the door, I noticed tiny, white flakes drifting down. The last thing we needed was more snow and cold. However, those were the two elements that winter typically liked to dish up in this state. Thankfully, my numerous layers of clothes kept me warm.

A fey walked down the sidewalk, carrying a box in his arms. He nodded at me when he saw me but didn't stop. My eyes stayed glued to what he carried. There was no mistaking the gigantic jar of pickles peeking out from the top of that box.

Without giving it a second thought, I began to follow. The dude walked fast, his long legs expanding the space between us. I had to work to keep up. My breath puffed out of me in small, white clouds. I don't know what outcome I was expecting by following him. A cache of food at the end of a rainbow? Maybe even a cookout in someone's backyard? Both dreams. Instead, the fey walked right up to someone's house and let himself inside.

Crap.

I pretended to keep walking as a light went on. Through the windows, I saw rows of shelving units. It didn't seem like someone's house but more of a—

I grinned and walked toward the house. Just as I reached the door, it swung open.

"Is this the supply shed?" I asked.

"Yes." The fey held the door for me and watched me closely for a moment before closing it.

I wasn't worried about him telling someone. I had permission to be in there. Granted, this wasn't my goal, but now that I was inside, I'd have a look. There was a table in the middle of the room that now held the box with the big pickle jar. Around the table were the shelves. Most of them were bare. But toward the back, there was still food. Plenty of food to feed me for over a week.

My mouth watered at the thought, and I set my hand on my belly. It gurgled and demanded it's due.

"I know you're hungry, baby dill. But we can't take this."

I thought back to the promise I'd made the baby growing inside of me. Before finding out I was pregnant, I hadn't been on a great path. Parties. Guys. Lots of alcohol. Some weed. It'd been a blast. However, my life had shifted the moment I took the pregnancy test. It'd been like a gong had gone off in my head, bringing a level of perspective I'd never had.

I'd realized just how much I wanted a baby. Someone to love, who would love me unconditionally in return. Or, at least, until it turned three. After that, I knew it'd be a gamble. However, none of those future hardships had scared me off.

I'd promised the baby I'd keep it safe and do everything in my power to give it an amazing life.

I hadn't counted on earthquakes, hellhounds, zombies, or the fey.

"When I made my promise, it wasn't just to keep you alive and safe. It was a promise to be a better person. A mom you'd be proud of. While stealing this food would make you very happy in the short term, it wouldn't make you proud in the long-term."

I walked along the rows of shelves and looked for the seeds that Mya had mentioned. Seeing cans of tuna fish and boxes of cheesy noodle dinners made my mouth water. Such a simple meal, and I would have given anything for it.

The seeds were tucked away near the back, close to several cases of empty canning jars. I looked through the box and pulled out a few packets that would grow quickly. Radishes and lettuce. Yum.

Having taken what I'd needed, I left the house. As I did, I noticed all the fey silently watching from the growing dark outside.

"Shadow ninjas," I said in awe.

One nodded to me, and I gave a quick smile in return before tucking my hands in my pockets and heading for Cassie's house.

When I reached her place, the lights were on and the curtains pulled closed.

Ignoring the "go away" vibe, I knocked on the front door. A familiar fey opened it only a few moments later.

"Hey, Kerr. Could I talk to Cassie please?"

"Come in." He stepped back to let me inside.

I willingly followed him into the kitchen. The scent of cooked meat drew me more than his welcoming smile. Not that there really was a smile.

Cassie sat at the table with her kids. One wiggled in a highchair. He couldn't have been more than a year old, if that. The other one, a girl, sat in a chair beside Cassie. Thanks to the tyke's booster seat, she could see the helping of noodles and stew on her plate. I tried to stay focused on the people and not the food.

"Well hi, Angel," Cassie said with a smile. "What brings you out tonight?"

"I was hoping I could talk to you for a minute. I'm sorry about interrupting your dinner." I tried not to drool as I spoke.

"Don't worry about it. Kerr, why don't you get Angel a chair?" He grunted and left the room. "You can join us," Cassie said as she placed a few chunks of cooked carrot on her son's tray. "It's more fun eating in a group than sitting in the house by yourself."

I was already halfway out of my jacket by the time she finished speaking.

"Thank you." There was no way I was stupid enough to say no to an invitation for food.

While Kerr looked for a chair, Cassie got me a plate. The extra-large serving she scooped out made me want to cry and cheer at the same time.

"Don't think I didn't notice how quickly you ate that casserole this morning," she said. "Don't be shy about eating as much as you need. If you run out of supplies, just let me know."

"About that. I don't have any supplies. I checked every inch of that house, and there's not a drop of food in it."

Cassie's face turned to one of shock.

"I am so sorry. I never thought to check."

Kerr returned with a chair and set it down next to the highchair. I sat and thanked him before turning to Cassie.

"I figured the lack of food was an oversight. It's no big deal."

"It is. You need a consistent diet. I'll have one of the fey bring a box over tonight."

I loaded a huge bite onto my fork and shoved it into my mouth. It was so good. For the next several minutes, I consumed their food. I tried to take it slow and drink between bites, but it wasn't easy.

"I'll see if I can't find you some dehydrated milk, too," Cassie said. "The food options we have aren't as rounded as you need."

"I don't mind. I'm happy with anything. I swear."

When I cleaned my plate, I set my fork down and actually took a moment to look at the other occupants. Kerr kept glancing at me. My table manners were probably horrible. Not that I really cared. I just wanted the food.

The little girl across from me smiled once she met my gaze.

"Hi," I said. "My name is Angel."

"My name is Lilly. That's my brother Caden. We thought he was dead."

"Um..." I looked at Cassie.

She looked just as startled by that last bit as I was.

"It's a miracle he's with us," Cassie said in quiet agreement. "Lilly's father's friend, Dawnn, kept Caden safe for us."

I recalled Cassie mentioning Dawnn from this morning.

"I'm glad he had her," I said.

"Me too."

The fact that there were still a few people out there willing to protect babies meant something. I wasn't ready to go shouting out that I was pregnant yet, but this made me feel a little bit better.

"Is Uncle Shax going to be coming over after dinner again?" Lilly asked.

"I'm not sure," Cassie answered.

"Uncle Shax?" I asked.

Cassie smiled slightly.

"Kerr calls all the fey his brothers. The title seemed appropriate."

"He comes over a lot?"

"Caden is a bit of a novelty," she said, reaching over to wipe her son's chin. "The fey have never seen a baby before."

The baby moved inside of me, a reminder of my ticking clock. The fey would be in for one hell of a shock in a few weeks.

CHAPTER FIVE

I HUMMED, DRANK THE REST OF THE MILK IN MY BOWL, THEN poured myself a third helping.

"This is the life, little lucky charm." I patted my pleasantly full belly then poured more milk.

I never thought I'd see milk again. It didn't matter that it was reconstituted from powder. It tasted like the real thing. At least, as much as I could remember the taste of the real thing. I figured it'd been almost eight weeks since the quakes. It wasn't easy to keep track, though.

I took another large bite of breakfast and took my time chewing. Last night, one of the fey dropped off a box filled with food. A lot of food. I didn't know where it came from because I'd seen what was in the storage shed and a lot of what I'd received wasn't what had been there. Not that I cared. Food was food, and I was grateful. And, being well fed yesterday sure made today's meal more enjoyable. I could eat slower.

The edge of my hunger was gone for the most part, which probably had something to do with the fact that I knew there was more food in my immediate future. I glanced at the cupboard still hanging open so I could stare at the nice supply of food in there. Enough for three square meals for four days.

The fey who had dropped off the food had assured me he would be back in three days with more food. Well before I ran out. I smiled and took another bite. I knew coming to Tolerance was a good idea.

The door to the kitchen flew open, startling my half-chewed bite out of my mouth. The glob fell to the table with a splat.

"What the hell, Shax?"

"She will not talk to me." He strode into the room, closed the door with another bang, and took off his jacket. I didn't mind his intrusion, just the loss of food. It was nice having his company. And his drama, as sad as it was for him, kept me from going completely crazy with boredom.

"Sit down and tell me what happened," I said. I got up to fetch the washcloth from the sink and cleaned up my mess while he sat.

"I did what you said. I spent quality time with my Hannah, and it did not work."

"Hold on. Backup. Tell me exactly what you did for your quality time and exactly how she responded."

I rinsed the washcloth out and sat back at the table. While he talked, I continued to eat.

"It was nice. I went to her house and just listened. She told me about her time before the earthquakes. She misses that life very much. She misses her family very much. I know more about Hannah, now. When she ran out of things to say, I offered to make her dinner. She said yes. So I knew I was being a good listener."

I hid my smile by wiping my mouth with a napkin.

"What did you make her for dinner?" I managed after a moment.

"Noodles with the red sauce that tastes awful. But I did not complain. I ate it. And she liked it. When we were finished, we watched a movie together. I did not ask to see her pussy. I did not ask for a kiss."

"Good job. What happened next?"

"While we watched the movie, I started to rub her feet like you showed me. She did not say no."

I couldn't wait to hear what happened next. Instead of talking, though, he growled slightly and pressed his hands down on the table.

"The suspense is killing me. Talk Shax. What happened?"

"I did what you said, but it didn't work."

He was going to make me waste my cereal on his head if he didn't tell me in the next two seconds.

"What exactly did you do?"

"She made a sound. When I was rubbing the bottom of her foot. It was a groan. A small one. So, I moved up a little. Not far. Just to her beautiful ankle. Her skin was so soft."

I could tell by the tone of his voice I was losing him.

"Stay with me, Shax. What happened next?"

"She pulled her foot away. When I asked her if she did not like the foot rub, she said she did, but she already knew where it was headed and did not want to go there. She said she has kissed me once already and does not intend to do so again. Then she told me I should leave. Now, this morning, she will not answer her door."

He looked at me accusingly like it was all my fault.

"That seems pretty final, Shax."

I looked down at my cereal and contemplated what to do next.

"Why would she say she does not want to kiss me again? Kissing is good."

"It can be, but maybe——"

I looked up at him.

"You need to kiss me like I'm Hannah."

His expression changed to one of complete horror.

"This is just for teaching and learning, Shax, like when I sat in your lap and made you grab my boobs." That just made him look more opposed to the idea. "Stop being a baby and just kiss me so I can tell you if it's good or not."

"If what is good?"

"Your kissing skills. Maybe that's why Hannah doesn't want to kiss you again. Maybe you're not a good kisser."

His expression changed ever-so-slightly, closing off. I'd just unintentionally hurt his feelings big time.

"Hey, don't worry about this. If the kissing isn't up to par, it's something we can work on. People can become great kissers. It's a skill that you can learn like any other."

He grunted and nodded, so I knew I had his consent.

"Before we get down to business, I need to brush my

teeth, so you don't taste my breakfast." I stood and hesitated, glancing at him.

"Do you guys brush your teeth? I mean, I'm not trying to be rude or anything. I just don't know what your hygiene routine is."

"Yes. Mya told us we must brush our teeth in the morning and at night."

"That's good."

I went off to brush my teeth, and when I returned, Shax was pacing the kitchen.

"Relax, big guy. Take a seat."

He grunted and sat on the kitchen chair which made him closer to my height. I moved toward him and nudged his legs apart so I could stand between them.

He watched me closely as if I was getting ready to bite his nose off instead of kiss him.

I set my hands on his shoulders and felt him tense. There was no way he'd kiss well when he was that nervous. I needed to distract him.

"Kissing isn't just about a physical connection of lips and tongue," I said. "It's an emotional one, too."

Some of the tension eased from his shoulder.

"For example, if both people aren't in the mood for a kiss, the kiss won't be great."

"How do I—?"

"Shh." I placed my finger over his lips.

"You're only allowed to listen and feel until we're done. You can ask questions afterwards, all right?"

He frowned and nodded.

"Besides, I already know what you were going to ask. You set the mood with words first." I let my gaze drift over his face. "You're a very handsome man, Shax. Any woman would be lucky to have you." I lifted a hand and trailed a finger along his jaw. "Strong yet kind." I traced his brow. "Amazing eyes." He blinked slowly, and I felt a shift in his mood. He was almost there.

I left his face to trace the edge of the ear poking from his hair.

"And adorable ears."

His jaw twitched as I played with the tip, and I knew I had him. When I leaned in, there was hunger in his gaze.

"Like I'm Hannah," I whispered just before my lips brushed his.

He hesitated a moment then his warm, firm lips pressed against mine. While he was imagining Hannah, I knew exactly who I was kissing. A tingle of excitement raced through me at the feel of his teeth and his hands as he gripped my arms.

I parted my lips and licked him lightly.

He growled and opened his mouth. I was lost to the touch and taste of him. He didn't kiss. He possessed. There was nothing tender in it, only raw need.

I threaded my fingers into his hair and held on for dear life, each thrust of his tongue stoking a fire within me that had been dormant for too long.

One moment I was standing between his legs and the next I was against a wall with my legs wrapped around his waist. I could feel every inch of the erection he had pressed against me. I groaned into his mouth and ground my hips against him.

Then, the baby kicked.

I broke the kiss and scrambled out of Shax's arms. He turned slowly to face me. His pupils were so dilated they almost looked humanly round instead of their normal slits.

We stared at each other, both breathing raggedly. I waited for his accusations. His gaze didn't dip to my belly, though.

Instead of speaking, he stepped toward me. I had no idea what to do. Was he going to yank up my shirt to make sure before he said anything?

I clenched my hands into fists and swore at my stupidity. Why had I thought the problem was with his skills? Everything the fey did was over the top amazing. Of course, Shax's kissing would be out of this world. Stupid, Angel. No. Stupid, Hannah. What the hell was wrong with that girl? I wanted to jump Shax on the spot.

He took another step, closing the distance and reaching for me.

"Shax, I don't know what to say," I said shakily.

Take me on the table was in close second to begging him not to tell anyone.

Before I could say either, and before he touched me, someone knocked on the door.

"Thank God," I said as I slipped around him and swung it open.

"Hey, Emily," I said when I saw who it was.

"Hey, Angel," she said in a rush. "I can't stay. I have to get to Hannah. I just stopped to tell you that something happened at Whiteman. A truckload of survivors just pulled up outside our wall. They're offloading people. Mya and Drav are already talking to them and splitting them up into groups. The survivors are staying here. In Tolerance. But, there's no way there's enough open houses for all of them. You're going to get company. Hide your food."

She looked over my shoulder briefly.

"Hey, Shax. You might want to check in with Mya and Drav."

Without another word, Emily turned around and rushed off down the sidewalk. I slowly closed the door then turned to face Shax.

He stood right behind me, his jacket already on. We looked at each other, the silence stretching. How could something that was meant to be so simple be so awkward?

"About what you felt," I said, knowing I needed to address it before he left.

"Is that how all kisses are supposed to feel?" he asked softly.

"The good ones," I said.

"That means I'm a good kisser?"

I smiled, realizing I was off the hook. He'd been so into the kiss, he hadn't noticed.

"If you kissed any better than that, you would have melted my panties off. Hannah's problem is definitely not the way you kiss. There's nothing wrong with your skills. We'll need to talk about this some more, but give me some time to think it over. I'm sure we'll come up with something. For right now, I think we need to figure out what's going on out there."

"We will talk later," he said with a nod.

He let himself out, and I basked in my reprieve for a moment before hurrying to my food supply.

I hadn't yet gotten rid of the box, so I started loading everything back in. There was no way I was going back to starving. Not when I got this food fair and square.

Once I had everything loaded in the box, I lugged it upstairs to my bedroom and hid it under my bed. Rushing back to the kitchen, I grabbed a piece of paper and some tape and scribbled "taken" in large letters. I slapped that sign on my bedroom door then grabbed my jacket on my way out.

It wasn't hard to figure out where to go. I followed the noise.

Mya and a few fey stood in the center of a cluster of people.

"If you guys can be patient just a little while longer," she said loudly, "we're working on figuring out where to put everyone. We need to clear a few of the fey out of their homes to make room. Everyone will have a bed to sleep in tonight."

Despite that amazing news, I still heard grumbles. People actually wondered why any of the fey needed houses when the cold didn't bother them in the first place. Assholes.

Mya saw me and nudged the woman beside her. After Mya pointed in my direction, the woman and a fey jogged my way.

"Hi, Angel. I'm Eden. I'm sorry to be the bearer of bad news, but you're going to get five to six roommates before the end of the day."

"That's okay," I said. "Do you know what's happening at Whiteman?"

"They had another fence breach, and it was pretty bad. The infected took out a whole section and actually dragged the fencing away. It won't be an easy repair even if it was worth the time to fix it. But, now that the infected know how to remove fencing, they'll just repeat the process as soon as it's up again.

"Matt knew it was time to move on. He had already found a new location not too far from here. Some of the fey have even been working on putting up a wall around it like the one we have here. Mya's sending half the fey over there, now, to help get it done faster and to make room for the Whiteman people here. Even with half the fey at the new location, there still won't be enough houses for all the survivors pouring in. This is just the first truckload."

"I seriously don't mind sharing the house."

"Good. She's assigning the number based on bathrooms. Three people per bathroom. Houses with two get six. Houses with three get twelve. It's going to get interesting."

"No doubt."

I glanced in the direction of the storage shed, my thoughts already going to food. There was no way we had enough supplies.

"Yeah, I know what you're thinking," Eden said. "With the fey focusing on the wall, it's going to be slim pickings for a little while. But, Matt and his men did manage to clear out the cafeteria, and they're returning the majority of the supplies we just sent them yesterday."

I nodded, but I didn't feel at all reassured.

"Thanks for the heads up. I labeled my door so anyone you send that way will know what rooms are open. I think I'll go see if I can help in the supply shed." More than anything, I just wanted to see how much food we were getting.

Eden and her fey jogged back to Mya, who was now writing down people's names and giving them house numbers.

Not wanting to hang around to see who I would be stuck with, I moved in the direction of the supply shed.

The door to the home was open, and a line of fey were already carrying boxes inside.

I slipped through the door, trying my best to stay out of everyone's way.

An older woman stood at the table, pulling things out of boxes and directing several fey where to put them. When she saw me, she smiled widely.

"You must be Angel. I'm Julie."

"Mya's mom, right?"

"Yep. I don't suppose you're here to help?"

"Sure. What can I do?"

She put me to work sorting through the supplies. Seeing the quantity of food coming in made me feel better. However, it also made me feel bad for Tolerance since they had sent so much to Whiteman and had kept so very little for themselves.

While we worked, a distant rumble of engines created a constant background noise. Even when the fey stopped coming in with boxes, the noise never stopped.

"Do you know how many people were living at

Whiteman?" I asked Julie. It wasn't anything that was ever announced as far as I knew.

"I think they were down to 447 last count. I don't know what it is after this recent break-in."

"How many people are coming here?"

"About 300. The rest will help the fey finish building the wall at the new location," she said.

I looked at all the food again. We'd be lucky if it lasted a week.

"Don't worry," she said. "As soon as the new wall is finished, the fey will go out on another supply run. They're good at finding what we need."

She seemed completely unconcerned with the incoming mouths and the lack of food to feed them.

"Let's line the empty boxes along the wall so we can start putting supplies in them. I like to do everything by threes. Three dinners. Three lunches. Three breakfast items. If we can fill fifty boxes with that, then we'll start adding more."

"What is this for?" I asked.

"Provisions to give each house. Since we don't do communal dining like they do over at Whiteman, the supplies are sent to each house without a fey provider. Most houses are going to have six to twelve people living in them. These rations won't seem like much, but it will be enough to let them know they're not going to starve here."

And it had worked on me.

Feeling depressed, I did as she asked. We worked side-by-side for the next several hours, sorting and filling boxes, only stopping for a small lunch break of pop tarts. Pure heaven.

As soon as we had all fifty of the boxes full, Julie called several fey in and gave them instructions to deliver the food to the new arrivals.

"One per house no matter what they say," she reminded them. "If there are any complaints, tell them to see Mya."

She shook her head and sighed.

"I hate that she has this burden when she's not feeling well."

"Eden's with her," I said. "I saw her helping."

"Good. You should get home. I don't know about you, but I'm ready to get off my feet."

"Sitting and some dinner doesn't sound like a bad idea," I said with a smile I didn't feel.

The truth was that I dreaded what was coming. After only a few days of freedom, I was back where I started. Just a different location.

How much longer would I be able to keep my secret while living with five other people?

CHAPTER SIX

I took my time getting back to the house. Everywhere I looked, there were more people than fey. And, not just because the humans now outnumbered them. No, the number of fey I saw walking around had significantly decreased because so many had already left to help with the new place.

Those who were still here watched the humans move around, staying out of their way. I wished I wasn't so afraid of drawing attention to myself. I wanted to wave, say hello, and be friendly to make up for the way the rest of my kind were ignoring them.

Instead, I saw Bertha coming out of a house and kept my head down as I continued walking. I didn't want these people to notice me. I didn't want them to remember that I'd left several days ago to come here, a place they thought I was stupid for wanting to go.

When I reached my house, every single light was on inside. I shook my head and let myself in.

The five people in the kitchen stopped what they were doing to look at me. Three people stood by the stove, and two already sat at the table. Despite the warmth, food, and safety, no one smiled. The room definitely gave off an unwelcome vibe. I'd probably startled them.

"Hi," I said, taking off my jacket. "I'm Angel."

No one said anything.

The two women by the counter gave me the stink-eye. The older one with the dark brown hair must have earned a gold medal for it at some point in her life. Ignoring them, I glanced at the guy by the stove. He seemed to have been waiting for me to look because he made a big deal out of scooping something onto a plate, which he passed to the first woman. She shook her head at me, accepted her plate, and took her spot at the table with the other two.

Maybe they'd lost someone with the last breach and resented me for being smart enough for leaving when I had.

"I'm sorry to hear about Whiteman," I said, trying to be nice.

"Yeah, I bet you were," the gold-medal glarer said. She took her plate from the man and sat down.

Not knowing what she meant by that, and not caring enough to ask, I went upstairs, figuring I'd give them some space to adjust to the new arrangements.

The door to my bedroom stood open, and the sign was missing. Someone's bag sat on my bed. I was torn between being annoyed and worried. How would I get my food out of there?

I looked over my shoulder at the sound of someone coming up the stairs. The champion glarer was there.

"Do you need something from my room?" she asked, crossing her arms.

I knew what a breach was like. The terror. The confusion. But how she was acting had nothing to do with the trauma she'd likely experienced earlier in the day. She was just being a dick for the sake of being a dick.

"Your room? I had a sign on the door. This is my room," I said, still trying to play nice.

"I didn't see a sign. Or any clothes to indicate anyone was staying here. I thought it was the supply room, given all the food under the bed."

She continued to glare at me. I didn't give any of my anger away even though I was raging inside. The woman's hateful attitude now made complete sense.

"No, it was my room, and that was my food."

"Your food? You mean our food. We don't keep individual rations."

I wanted to punch her in the face. The baby kicked. A convenient reminder of who I was supposed to be. These people were just as hungry as I was. As much as it sucked, I'd share.

"Fine. We share. What's for dinner?"

"You expect us to share with you when you wouldn't share with us? I don't think so. Oh, and you get the couch."

She turned her back on me and went downstairs.

Seething, I stood there for a minute. There really wasn't much I could do except cause a fight for a share of the food. I wasn't against physical violence when it was warranted. But the situation didn't call for it just yet. Not when I had other resources.

I went back downstairs and grabbed my jacket. No one said anything as I left again.

Outside, people were still milling about.

I walked down the street to Cassie's house and knocked on her door. I waited several minutes, but no one answered. Bummed, I considered what to do next. I briefly thought of Emily and Hannah, but if they were stuck with people, too, I didn't want to call attention to any food the pair might have successfully hidden away.

I didn't know anyone else. Not true. There was one other person who might be able to help me.

I waved to the nearest fey, who immediately jogged my way.

"Do you know where Shax lives?"

The fey gave me the house number and nodded when I thanked him. It only took a few minutes to get to Shax's. However, when I knocked at the door, I got the same non-answer as I did at Cassie's house.

Frustrated and hungry, I started back toward my house. The faint sound of an infected call echoed in the air. Slowing, I looked at the darkening sky. I hoped the infected had followed the survivors here rather than the presence of so many humans drawing them.

As the car lights came on one by one, the infected calls

grew louder. I glanced at a fey standing in the shadows and smiled at him. More than ever, we needed them. I hoped the people who arrived here today would remember that and be kinder than they were the last time we all lived together.

When I got back to the house, it was still lit up like a damn Christmas tree. I went inside and saw four of my five companions in the living room, watching a movie and eating a bowl of damn popcorn. That was definitely from my supplies. Angry didn't even touch how I felt. Pregnant lady hormones turned me into a green, raging monster, and I was ready to start smashing things.

"I'm tired," I said. "Since that's my bedroom you're sitting in, get out."

"You don't own this place," the woman who'd confronted me said.

"You've got ten seconds to get your ass upstairs in that bed, or I'm going to sleep in it," I said. "Ten...nine... eight..." I moved toward the stairs, and she stood and glared at me.

"Bring it, bitch," she said.

I fisted my hands and took a step toward her.

"I think we've all had a long day, Carol. It wouldn't be a bad idea to turn in," a voice said from behind me.

I stopped and glanced back at one of the guys who'd been sitting at the kitchen table. He didn't glare at me like the rest. In fact, his gaze didn't shift to me at all but remained locked on Carol.

"Are you seriously sticking up for her?" Carol demanded.

He exhaled heavily and shook his head. Disappointed, I faced the group as he continued to talk.

"Turn off the TV and use your ears. Can you hear the infected out there? It's better to get sleep now, when we can, because we don't know how long this wall will keep them out."

That seemed to motivate the group. The other three stood and left the room. Carol glared at me and eventually took her popcorn and left.

When I turned to watch her go upstairs, the younger guy was gone, and I was alone. All the anger left me as I moved to the couch. Without a pillow or any bedding other than the blanket already there, I laid down. What a shitty day. Roommates. No food. At least it was warm. And a couch was better than sleeping in a tent on a cot.

I closed my eyes and planned on a better day once I woke up. However, I wasn't sure I ever got to sleep.

I tossed and turned a lot, an ever-increasing ache consuming my back. The sky was lightening when I finally gave up and went to use the bathroom.

When I reemerged, Carol was sitting at the kitchen table. She looked like hell. Her hair was a tangle, and her eyes were half-closed. But she still managed to watch me closely as I went to the fridge.

"What the hell do you think you're doing?" she asked.

"Get over yourself. I'm drinking some milk."

"That's not your milk."

"And it's not yours, either. Remember? We don't get personal rations. It's all shared."

I poured myself a glass and heard her stand, already knowing what was coming. When her hand closed over my left wrist, I grabbed the milk glass with my right and slammed down the contents before she could stop me.

She slapped me across the face before I finished the last swallow. The glass clanked against my teeth and flew into the cupboard, where it shattered. Milk dribbled down my chin as we glared at each other. Bitch crossed a fucking line.

I closed my fist and showed her how it was done. Even underfed and pregnant, I still had enough strength to make her jaw joint crack.

Feet came tromping down the stairs as she cried out.

"What the hell is going on?" an older man demanded.

"Carol didn't want me drinking a glass of milk," I said. "Apparently shared rations doesn't really mean shared."

"She fucking tried hiding her food from us, Harry." Carol sounded nasally when I hadn't even hit her nose.

"Drama queen," I said.

Her head whipped toward me, and Harry stepped between us.

"You both need to cool off. Angel, you should leave."

"Why the hell should I leave? I was here first."

"Because you threw a punch."

"She slapped me." I gestured to my flaming cheek.

"Get your jacket and get out," he said with finality.

And that is why I knew I was fucked once people found out I was pregnant. There was no mercy, no consideration in humanity anymore.

I grabbed my jacket and left the house just as the sun was rising.

No more than five steps from the door, I heard someone call my name. I looked up and found Shax walking toward me.

"I was coming to talk to you," he said. "Are you leaving?"

I sighed, knowing the situation would escalate if I didn't handle things correctly. The fey didn't tolerate any abuse of a woman, whether the woman was claimed by one of them or not.

"Yeah, I needed a bit of fresh air," I said with a smile.

He frowned as he joined me.

"Why is there a mark of a hand on your cheek?" He growled low as he continued to study me. "Did someone slap you?"

I started walking in the direction of the storage shed. There was one package of pop tarts left in the box from yesterday, and I didn't care what anyone said about sharing. That package had my name on it.

Shax kept pace with me, and I waited until we reached the end of the block to explain.

"It was another girl," I said.

He continued to frown.

"It was a teaching and learning moment."

"What were you teaching?"

"Violence breeds violence," I said with a wide smile that hurt my cheek. "That means I hit her back. A lot harder than she hit me. She'll think twice before trying to start a fight with someone she doesn't know."

He grunted.

In the silence following his grunt, I heard raised voices.

"Did you hear that? It sounds like arguing."

Another grunt. I grinned.

The further we walked, the louder the voices became. I could almost make out the words when Shax glanced at me.

"You should go home, Angel."

"What? No way."

"It might not be safe."

"It's safe enough. Those are human voices, not infected calls. And, just because someone's arguing doesn't mean they're fighting. Besides, I just told you I know how to throw a punch."

He frowned at me.

"Mya says we are not supposed to hit humans."

"That's because you're fey, and you could cause a lot of damage. I'm human, so I get to hit my own kind."

I grinned at him. He was not amused.

When we turned the corner, we saw people gathered around the storage shed. Men and women, survivors from Whiteman, faced off with a group of fey led by Mya.

"You have no right to wall us in and starve us," someone yelled.

"You're not walled in," Mya said. "You can climb up any one of the ladders the fey have put out for you and leave anytime you please. And when the fey guarding the top of the wall see you returning, they will help you get back in."

"We'll die out there," another person yelled.

"There's food in that building. There's no reason for us to leave Tolerance," a third yelled.

"We need to eat," a new voice chimed in.

"And you have eaten," Mya said, her annoyance showing. "Each one of the houses you're staying in had a food delivery last night. If you don't know how to ration what you were given, that's not my fault."

"Ration? That wasn't enough to feed twelve people two meals."

I wanted to snort. I'd packed those boxes. Julie had ensured there was enough for nine, twelve-person meals in the boxes going to the houses with three bathrooms. Either, like me, they had crappy roommates who weren't sharing, or they ate it all thinking it'd be easy to get more now that they lived with the fey again.

"You've got us crammed in those houses like sardines," someone else yelled.

People were obviously worked up about their new lives. The idiots couldn't see how great it really could be.

"You're welcome to go back to the tents," Mya said. "No one is keeping you here."

"Give us the fucking food," yet another person yelled, which incited even more yelling.

Beside me, Shax growled.

"Go home, Angel."

He jogged toward the crowd and joined the fey keeping the humans from entering the storage shed.

This standoff was the last thing both sides needed. I should have been upset by the survivor's stupidity and displays of hostility. Instead, I was more upset that I wouldn't get my damn Pop-Tarts. It seemed that no matter where I lived, my future would involve some sort of starvation.

One of the humans threw something at one of the fey. The one standing beside Mya roared. She looked ready to explode, too.

"You know what? Everything that's in this house is yours," Mya shouted. "And when it's out, it's out. Not a single fey is going to bring back supplies for any of you. You're on your own."

She led the fey away, and the humans rushed for the supply shed.

I turned around and walked back the way I'd come.

A few people ran past me with boxed meals or canned goods clutched in their hands. They were too stupid to see they'd burned a bridge. Without the fey's help on supply runs, they were going to get a lot hungrier. I was going to get a lot hungrier, too.

I went to the only welcoming house I knew and felt bad for knocking on Cassie's door. Given the hour, I did it quietly just in case the kids were still sleeping.

Kerr opened the door with his usual stoic face. It didn't put me off. That seemed to be the fey's normal expression most of the time.

"Hey, Kerr. I'm really sorry to bother you this early, but could I talk to Cassie, please?"

"I'm here," Cassie said from somewhere inside.

Kerr stepped aside, and I saw Cassie right there, holding

her son. She passed the boy off to Kerr and greeted me with a smile.

Behind her, Kerr didn't move.

"Would you like to go for a walk?" I asked.

Cassie glanced at Kerr then chuckled.

"Sure. Let me just get my boots on."

I waited until she was outside and the door was closed.

"Let's go to the backyard," I said, already moving that way. "It's probably safer than walking around right now."

"What do you mean?" Cassie asked, leaving new prints in the fresh snow with me.

"I was just at the storage shed. There was a huge blowout between Mya and some of the survivors."

"Is Mya okay?"

We rounded the corner to the back of the house.

"Yeah, everyone's fine. But, all of the rations are gone. People were pissed that they didn't get more. So, they took everything. Mya told them that once it's gone, it's gone. The fey weren't going to bring in any more supplies. The humans need to fend for themselves."

I lowered my voice.

"I don't know what to do, Cassie. I can't feed myself. How am I supposed to feed this baby when it gets here?"

I set my hand on my stomach.

"He kicks when I eat or when I'm extremely emotional but doesn't move much in between. I don't want this baby to die before it even has a chance to live."

Cassie pulled me into a hug.

"We won't let that happen," she said fiercely before

releasing me. "I think it's time we let Mya in on what's going on. You're not like these other survivors who are asking for too much. And once these fey know that you're pregnant, they will do everything they can to help. We need to let people know."

"Not yet," I begged. "There has to be another way. You didn't see how they—"

Something crunched behind me at the same time Cassie's eyes widened.

I spun around.

Shax stood there, his hands loose at his side, and his gaze pinned on my middle.

"Pregnant," he said softly.

His gaze lifted, meeting mine. Then, he smiled so wide I saw his gum line.

CHAPTER SEVEN

"We were talking about when Cassie was pregnant with Caden," I lied quickly.

Shax stalked toward me, his gaze locking on my baby bulge once more.

"No, you were not. I was listening. You are pregnant. That means you have a baby inside of you."

"Shax, you know you're not supposed to listen in on other people's conversations. Mya talked to you about that," Cassie said.

He waved his hand like it didn't matter, his gaze completely focused on my belly.

"When will it come out?" he asked. "I would like to see how small a baby starts out."

Behind him, I spotted another fey. The guy was just walking between yards, minding his own business—like Shax should have been. But the fact that we were out in the open, and one fey had already overheard what he shouldn't have, had me clapping a hand over Shax's mouth.

"Let's talk about this, but not here. Somewhere private. Okay?"

He picked me up, and I squealed and tried to get out of his arms.

"Wait," Cassie said. "Take her inside. You can use Caden's room."

She opened the back door, and Shax carried me in. I should have been grateful she'd stopped him from carrying me off to who knew where, but I was still freaking out that he knew my secret.

He raced upstairs and closed us into a bedroom.

Placing me on my feet, he began to unzip my jacket. I batted his hands away.

"Shax, stop."

"I want to see."

"Well, you can't."

"Why not?"

He knelt before me and tilted his head as if he suddenly had x-ray vision and could see through all my layers.

"Can it hear me? Is it a boy like Caden or a girl like Lilly?"

"I don't know. Shax, get up. We need to talk. You can't tell anyone about this."

That got his attention. His gaze flew to mine; and for a long moment, he just stared at me.

"We will make a new deal," he said. "I will keep the secret, and you will let me see the baby."

"First, that's not a deal. That's blackmail. Second, you can't see it when it's still inside me."

In his frustration, he made a face that was completely adorable.

"It is not blackmail. If both parties get what they want in a fair trade, it is a deal. You want my silence. I want..." He reached out to grab my shirt again.

I dodged his hand.

"I don't care. Making deals with you sucks. I gave you a ton of advice about what girls want in a guy, and I got a lousy, small bag of chips in return because you thought I was too fat. You still need to pay up from our first deal."

"I will pay up. Then, we will make a new deal. You will tell me everything you know about the baby, and I will not tell anyone."

"Deal," I said quickly.

He frowned. "How much do you know about the baby?"

"Not much," I said reluctantly.

"Then it is not fair. You must also let me touch you while it is growing inside you."

"Deal." I didn't mind a few belly touches. In fact, I couldn't wait to see Shax's face the first time he could feel the baby kick. He would flip out.

He reached for me again, but I stopped.

"Uh-uh. First, you pay up for the advice. Then, you can start touching."

He made that frustrated face again, and I grinned.

"We keep things fair this time."

He grunted and got to his feet.

"And remember, Shax. No one can know."

"It will take me some time to find some food. I gave what I had to Mya to give the other humans so they would stop fighting."

Damn selfish jerks continued to block me from eating.

"I think I'm going to go back to my house then. I'll check in with you tomorrow, okay?"

"Okay. But no more teaching and learning." He ran a gentle finger over my cheek.

"I'll do my best."

He gave my belly another longing look and followed me as I left the room. At the bottom of the steps, I hesitated. I could hear Cassie and her family still in the kitchen. I knew I should go tell her that everything was okay now. At least, I thought it would be okay with Shax's help. Not that he knew he was going to help me. I knew how badly he wanted to touch my belly, though. Hopefully, it was bad enough to keep me stocked in food.

Did I feel guilty about not clarifying that I meant to use his obsession to keep me fed? No. Like he said, it would be a fair trade. As soon as he wasn't interested anymore, I would have to find another way to feed myself.

So, given the nature of our deal and my unspoken hopes for it, I skipped checking in with Cassie and went straight for the front door.

Outside, Shax took off at a run without a word. I had no idea where he was going but hoped it was to raid some secret stash of food somewhere.

I made my way slowly back to the house. There were fewer people outside, now. Probably because news had spread that the spare supply of food was already claimed, and those who still needed food knew there wasn't anything left. I wondered how many people were going to brave going outside the wall and how many would wait in the homes, slowly starving until the fey caved. Because, they would. At least, for the women they would.

When I let myself into the house I now had to share, the TV was on again; and the kitchen smelled faintly like brown sugar oatmeal.

My stomach growled.

I slammed the door, ticked at them and the apocalypse in general.

At the sound, someone stood in the living room. It was the young guy from the night before. He came into the kitchen and took a covered bowl out of the microwave. I started salivating.

"We saved you your share of oatmeal," he said.

"This is how you share. You don't keep it all for yourself," Carol yelled from the other room.

"Thanks for thinking of me, Carol. I hope the oatmeal was easy for you to chew this morning."

The woman swore and stomped off upstairs.

I grinned and sat down at the table. The guy uncovered the bowl and got me a spoon.

"I'm Garrett, by the way."

I spooned in my first bite and almost groaned. It was brown sugar oatmeal.

"Thanks for not being a jackass like the others, Garrett," I said after I swallowed.

"We can hear you," Harry said.

"That was the point." I took another bite.

Garrett sat next to me.

"We don't know how long we're going to be in forced cohabitation," he said. "It would be better for everyone if we tried to get along." As he spoke, he wasn't looking at me but at the living room. Yet, I knew what he said applied to me as well. And he was right. Poking at the soft spots would just make them angrier and, in the long run, my life more miserable.

After I finished my breakfast and washed my dishes, I discovered there wasn't any more food left. Nothing. Like every other house, my roommates seemed to have eaten it all. Instead of asking what they were thinking, or calling them out for being the idiots they were, I went back to the basement and started planting the seeds.

No one bothered me down there. They'd probably already seen the snake body. It was hard to miss in the center of the floor. I figured I'd already killed one, though, so I could do it again.

With the bat close by, I worked on creating a future food supply, which kept me busy for several hours. With the bedrooms taken and the living room an unwelcoming environment, I stayed in the basement and found myself a chair to watch my plants grow.

Near dinner-time, Garrett called for me. I jerked myself awake, not surprised boredom had put me to sleep.

"Coming," I called, getting up and stepping around the dehydrating pile of goo that used to be the snake.

"What's up?" I asked when I reached the top.

"There's someone at the door for you."

I looked at the door and saw Shax. Worried that he would say something or do something to give me away, I hurried toward him.

"Would you like to come to my house?" he asked. He held out my jacket and leaned toward me.

"I have food," he said quietly.

I grabbed my jacket from his hands and slipped it on.

"Let's go."

As soon as I stepped outside the door, Shax scooped me up into his arms.

"Cut it out," I said, squirming to get free. "People are going to wonder what's going on."

"No one will wonder. My brothers will know I am lucky, and the humans will believe you are a lazy traitor to your own kind."

I snorted a laugh and stopped struggling. He'd summed that up pretty well.

A minute later, he set me down outside of his house and opened the door for me.

I stepped inside his entry and looked around. The living room had a leather sofa and recliner along with a huge TV. Beyond that, there was a breakfast bar that separated the living room from the kitchen.

"Is there anyone else here?" I asked.

"No. I live here alone."

"How is it you get a house all to yourself?" I took off my jacket and hung it in the coat closet.

"The humans did not want to live with the fey, and my brothers know I am close to winning a female."

I nodded, feeling kind of guilty that I hadn't considered Hannah in all of the deal-making I was doing with Shax. Rather than ask about Hannah or how he felt about keeping secrets from her, I asked about something else I found extremely important.

"What did you find for me to eat?"

He withdrew an individual snack cake from his pocket and held it out to me. It was mashed nearly flat and so small. That was my dinner? The healthy finish to an already crappy day of eating? How was I supposed to live on a cup of oatmeal, a pop tart, and a snack cake?

I looked up at him, fighting to keep the tears back.

"Do you know how hard it is to grow a baby? How much energy it takes? A lot. I'm tired and hungry all the time. But there's not enough food. Sure as hell not enough healthy food. If I don't eat enough, the baby dies. It's that simple."

I snatched the cake from him and ripped it open. Choking on my tears, I took a bite, barely chewing before swallowing. I tried telling myself to be grateful for anything, but the sudden overwhelming self-pity flooding me wouldn't listen.

I silently cried and ate my cake.

"Stay here," Shax said. A moment later he was gone, not even shutting the door behind him.

"Where else would I go?" I asked the empty room.

I sighed and closed the door. It wasn't like I wanted to go back to my house and sit in the basement like a pariah.

While I waited, I looked around Shax's house. Second by second, the feelings of frustration and anger faded as quickly as they'd welled up.

"Damn hormones," I said, throwing the wrapper away in the kitchen. I'd probably freaked Shax out with my crying. Well, he wanted to know everything about growing a baby; and apparently, he was going to get the crash course version.

I continued wandering through his house, looking at the home he'd made for himself. And I was shamelessly nosey doing it. He had a wide variety of clothes stashed in the master bedroom dresser. In one of the other rooms, he had a baby crib set up with a ton of baby toys.

"Holy shit," I said. I'd never seen a man who wanted a baby as much as Shax acted like he wanted one.

The door opened downstairs.

"Angel?" he called.

"Coming," I answered, leaving the nursery quickly.

I jogged down the stairs and found him in the kitchen. He was taking a pot out and filling it with water.

"What's going on?" I asked.

He turned and looked at me with worry in his eyes.

"I will cook some food for you. The baby will not die."

"Oh, Shax…I'm really sorry for scaring you like that. The baby isn't in immediate danger of dying. I'm eating. Maybe not as much as I would like or what I should, but I'm getting food just like everyone else. Food is scarce now. I shouldn't have cried about it."

I sat at the kitchen table.

"Remember how you wanted to know more about growing a baby? Well, my little outburst and tears? That's part of growing a baby. It's hormones. They go up and down like crazy. One minute I'm fine, and the next minute I'm crying or laughing or whatever. The point is I might get spontaneously emotional, and it doesn't necessarily mean something's wrong. It just means I'm growing a baby."

He considered me for a moment.

"Would the baby grow better with more food?"

I shrugged a little.

"That's probably a better question for Cassie. She knows more than I do. This is my first time being pregnant."

I didn't want to freak him out any more than I already had with Cassie's concerns about my weight gain. She'd know better how to deal with Shax's questions.

"So where did you find that?" I asked, nodding toward the box dinner he was preparing. Not only did he have that, but he also had a small can of chicken to add to it.

"I went to Hannah's house. She wouldn't talk to me, but Emily did. She was willing to make a deal. It was a fair trade."

I felt a little bad that he had gone to Hannah's, and she still wouldn't even talk to him.

"Hey, have I ever told you about pick-up lines? They're great icebreakers and an easy way to start a conversation with someone you like. They're usually meant to be funny while still showing your interest in the other person. Maybe that's what Hannah needs. A little less intensity and a little more humor."

He turned away from me and started opening the can.

"For example, do you know the essential difference between sex and conversation?"

He stopped opening the can and glanced at me with a puzzled look.

"No?" I asked with a grin. "Do you wanna go upstairs and talk?"

He didn't crack a smile.

"Get it? If you don't know the difference between sex and conversation, when I ask if you want to go upstairs to talk, I'm actually hoping to trick you into sex."

He grunted and went to the sink to drain the can.

"Okay. Let's try another one. Do you sleep on your stomach? If not, can I?"

"I will not ask Hannah these questions."

"Oh, come on. These are gold. I'm telling you pick-up lines are a great way to break the ice."

"Tell me more about hormones."

"There's not much I know about them other than they're a pain in the ass. It's hard not to be a hot mess with them. During the apocalypse? It's impossible. I once saw an infected with his eye dangling from the socket and laughed because it reminded me of those googly eyes I used in preschool."

I yawned suddenly.

"Sorry. Naps and early bedtimes are also a thing when pregnant."

He poured the noodles into the steaming water.

"And I hear I'll start walking with a waddle during my third trimester. That's why I wanted to come here. Running was already getting hard. And keeping my pregnancy secret would have been impossible in Whiteman."

"Why don't you want others to know?"

"Because people are scared. Many survivors see babies as a resource leech. A person who uses supplies but doesn't do any work to give back."

"Babies give joy and hope," Shax said.

I smiled.

"I guess they do. They also give pregnant women spontaneous flatulence. You've been warned."

He grunted and continued to make dinner while I threw every useless fact I knew at him. It wasn't much.

"Seriously, I don't know much. Cassie probably knows a ton more."

He set a plate in front of me, heaping with gravy, noodles, chicken, and bits of vegetables.

"Eat."

My mouth watered, and I picked up the fork. An idea formed before I took the first bite.

"Let's turn on the TV and sit in the living room."

He didn't stop me when I carried my plate to the couch and set it down. While he picked out a movie, I went around and closed all the curtains. Once I knew we would have privacy, I stripped down to just one shirt and sat on the couch. He watched me closely, his intense gaze on my stomach.

I patted the cushion beside me.

"Sit by me. I want to show you what happens when I eat."

He sat, and I took one hand and placed it on my belly. He made a slight noise in the back of his throat and moved his hand over my small bulge.

"Just wait. It gets better," I said.

Then, I started eating.

It didn't take the little ninja long to start moving. The first kick centered a little low under my belly button. I waited, and typical ninja-style, the baby suddenly kicked under my ribs.

The moment the baby kicked Shax's idly roaming hand was priceless. The big guy froze, and his eyes widened.

I grinned and took another bite.

The baby kicked him again. A wide smile spread over his face, and his other hand settled on my stomach.

CHAPTER EIGHT

"It's getting late. I should really get going." I covered my yawn with my hand. I'd been doing it almost nonstop since I finished my last bite of food.

Shax grunted in acknowledgment but didn't remove his hands from my belly. To say he was obsessed was an understatement.

I grabbed my plate and stood.

"Don't worry. The baby's going to be in there for a while. Lots of kicking opportunities in the future."

He grunted and followed me into the kitchen.

"Thanks for dinner, Shax. It was amazing."

"I will have more food tomorrow," he said.

I smiled and turned around to give him a hug. This time, his arms didn't hesitate to wrap around me.

"Thank you. For caring and for keeping my secret. It's a scary enough world to live in without worrying about people wanting to kick me out."

His arms tightened around me.

"No one will make you leave."

I patted his back and pulled away.

"I hope you're right."

He hovered as I put all my layers on again.

"Do babies make you cold?" he asked.

"Just the opposite, I think. I wear the layers to hide my belly. It gets a little hot sometimes."

He grunted and didn't say anything more as I shrugged into my jacket and waved goodbye. But he did take a step like he would come with me.

"It'd be better if I walked home alone. You don't want word getting back to Hannah that you're hanging out with another girl. It'll make my job harder. I'll see you tomorrow, though, right?"

He nodded and watched me leave.

Outside, the car lights were already on. Several people randomly walked from house to house, knocking on doors to ask for food from other survivors. There were a few raised voices before I made it home.

When I opened the door, Garrett was sitting at the kitchen table. The rest of the house was dark.

"Where is everyone?" I asked.

"Up in their rooms. I found the battery bank. With the clouds, we need to change how we're using the electricity and start turning things off."

My eyes went to the basement door.

"Don't worry. Those are the only lights that will stay on all the time. Actually, those little plants are the reason for the change. I removed the snake, too, by the way."

I took off my jacket and hung it up. It sucked that they'd found the planters and lights. The deal with Shax kept me fed now, but what about in a month? Yet, I wasn't overly upset the others knew. Those few pots wouldn't have been enough. They were a band-aid at best.

"Make sure to point out to bitchzilla that I wasn't hiding them. They were in the open in the only space available to me."

"We saved you some dinner," he said, not acknowledging my comment. Or maybe he was just trying to avoid a fight.

He went to the microwave and removed a small bowl of plain noodles. It wasn't much, but I had a feeling, this time, it was an equal share of what they'd had for dinner.

"Thank you," I said. "But I already ate somewhere else. You can have it."

He glanced down at the bowl.

"I'm glad you found something. This isn't much to live on."

"No. It's not. I think I'm going to get ready for bed."

When I re-emerged from the bathroom, the kitchen was empty. I turned off the light and took my place on the couch. Garrett had left me a pillow. Sure as hell wouldn't have been anyone else in the house.

Even with the pillow, I slept fitfully. The cupboard door slamming around dawn jolted me out of a semi-decent doze.

"Carol, you know there's no food in there," Garrett said.

"She might have hidden some more," she said.

I rolled my eyes behind my closed lids.

"I doubt that."

"If we want to eat, we need to go outside the wall and look for supplies," Harry said. "There's a group heading out this morning to go through Warrensburg. What the group finds, they divide between the people who help. At least two of us should go along. It's safer in numbers."

"Send her," Carol said.

I didn't need my eyes open to know she meant me.

"No. We're not forcing anyone," Garrett said. "I've been to Warrensburg before and know the areas the Whiteman supply runs have already touched. I'll go. And what I bring back, I'll share with everyone in this house."

"Your risk, your way," Harry said even as Carol swore and slammed another door.

"Let her sleep," Garrett said.

"Why? Why should she get more sleep than any of the rest of us?"

"Maybe because I'm the one sleeping on the crappy couch." I got up and started folding the blanket.

"That's on you for being selfish."

"So, the broomstick up your ass is your punishment for what?"

She actually tried coming after me. Harry stepped in front of her and glared at me.

"I know. I know. It's all my fault, and I should leave again until Carol can pull her shit together."

I walked past them to get my jacket.

"It was people like you who cost my daughter her life," Carol accused, her face red with her rage.

"We've all lost someone. Whatever anger you feel is because of your regrets and has nothing to do with me."

She went completely still, her eyes wide like I'd slapped her. Then, she lunged for me. I left while Harry was holding her back.

The sun was barely up when I stepped outside. I set out in the direction of Shax's house. There weren't many people moving around, yet. Probably because they were sane, unlike the people in my house.

Tired from a crappy night's sleep, I shuffled along the sidewalks and nodded to the occasional fey I spotted. I didn't know what I was expecting when I reached Shax's house, but it definitely wasn't the no-answer I received.

I really had nowhere else to go, and it was cold as hell outside. I wasn't just going to walk around forever because Carol had a stick up her butt. I understood she lost someone, but I meant what I'd said. We'd all lost someone at some point. I was born with parents, but I had no idea where they were. I was a realist and figured they were probably dead like all of my other relations.

I knocked again, a little bit more aggressively, and when I still got no answer, I tried the knob. It turned under my hand, and the door opened.

"Shax?" I called, stepping in and closing the door behind me.

"If you're up there sleeping in the buff, you might want to put something on because you have company."

There was still no noise. No movement.

I took off my jacket and kicked off my shoes, hoping that Shax wouldn't mind if I borrowed a bed for a while. There were three rooms in this place after all. I went upstairs and picked the guest bedroom, which had a full-size bed with a nice, comfy quilt.

I was out the moment I covered up.

"IT IS NOT A BAD WORLD. And I will keep you safe. You should come out, now."

The sound of Shax's voice had been niggling at my consciousness for a while. But it was that last gently-worded demand that woke me.

I rubbed my eyes and lifted my head. Shax was lying beside me. Sort of. His head was next to my belly, and his legs hung off the bed. Apparently, he was having a conversation with the ninja.

"He can't come out now," I said. "He needs to stay in there until he's done growing."

"He? Is it a boy?"

"I told you...I don't know. It just makes more sense to call him a 'he' or a 'she' rather than 'it.' 'It' seems so impersonal."

Shax's hand, which had been warming the side of my belly, moved in a gentle circle over the whole surface. It took a moment to register his hand was on my skin, not on my shirt.

"Making yourself right at home, I see," I said.

"You, too."

He had me there.

"Yeah, sorry about just coming in and grabbing a bed. I'm sleeping on the couch at my house, and it's starting to hurt my back."

"I liked finding you here."

I chuckled. Given how Shax had made himself comfortable with my belly, I bet he had.

"Want to learn how to give a pregnant lady a backrub?" I asked.

"Yes. But I do not have more food yet."

Guilt hit me hard.

"This isn't part of the trade. This is just me teaching you something that will make me feel good. Purely selfish on my part. But it's a skill that any girl would appreciate you knowing. Still want to learn?"

"Yes."

I grinned and rolled to my side.

As soon as I pointed out where to rub, he didn't need any further instruction. His fingers were heaven, and I was groaning within seconds.

"What should I do when you groan?" he asked.

"Just keep going. Don't ever stop when you get the girl groaning. She might die."

He started rubbing more frantically, edging toward my sides which sent me into a fit of laughter.

"Stop! Stop! I'm going to pee!" I gasped out between laughs.

"But you groaned. You said you would die."

"It was an exaggeration. The peeing will be real."

He stopped what he was doing, and it took me a few moments to catch my breath.

"I'm sorry. I forgot you guys take some things literally. If I groan, you can stop. I probably just won't like it when you do. I won't actually die because of it."

"Did you pee?" he asked.

"I don't know...do you have a washing machine?"

He gave me an odd look.

"I'm kidding. I'm fine. But in a few weeks, tickling me will be dangerous. I sneezed the other day and had a bit of a problem."

"Can I try rubbing your back again?"

"Heck yes. I should have warned you when we started out that lots of people are very ticklish on their sides. The closer you get to the armpits, the worse it gets. I don't know why that is."

I rolled over to my side again, and he immediately started rubbing the spot that had made me groan. It felt so good. I couldn't remember the last time someone had given me a backrub.

"So where were you this morning?" I asked.

"Some of the humans from Whiteman are leaving for a supply run today. I was helping them over the wall."

"Yeah, I heard about the supply run. I think a few people from my house are going."

Shax grunted and kept rubbing. The way his fingers seemed to find every knot almost made me drool.

"This gives new meaning to the term 'Friends with

Benefits,'" I said. "I could get really used to being your friend, Shax."

"New meaning? What is the old meaning?"

"Friends with Benefits is used to describe two people who are just friends, who help each other out in special ways as well. Usually they're helping each other out sexually. But, with no strings attached."

"What does 'no strings attached' mean?"

"It means that they're doing it without expecting any type of compensation or payback."

"I will be your friend with benefits."

I grinned.

"Oh? And what benefits are you hoping for?"

Given his infatuation with Hannah, I knew it couldn't be sex.

"I would like the baby to be mine when it is out."

"You can't have my baby, Shax," I said kindly.

"Why not?"

"Because I want my baby."

"Cassie is sharing Caden with Kerr."

"I think their situation is a little different. They're a couple. We're not."

I rolled to my back, and he immediately started feeling my belly.

"I think you need to try with Hannah again. Does she know how much you want a baby? Have you ever talked to her about it? You could try starting a conversation about Caden and see what she thinks about babies. You never know where the conversation might lead. If you're lucky, maybe you'll be able to use one of those pickup lines I taught you."

He didn't say anything, just continued to rub my belly, and I knew I needed to be the one to get up if I wanted to motivate him.

He made a grumping noise when I stood but let me be.

"While you're at Hannah's can I use your shower?"

"Yes."

He didn't leave.

I rolled my eyes, took him by the hand and led him downstairs. I even had to hand him his jacket and push him out the door.

"Go. You'll be fine," I said.

I closed the door on him and shook my head before making my way back upstairs.

Since he didn't mind that I'd helped myself to a bed, I also helped myself to one of his large, button up shirts and a pair of string tied shorts so I'd have something to wear when I was clean. I didn't linger in the shower just in case things worked out, and he returned with Hannah. Even fast, the shower was amazing.

Clean and wearing Shax's clothes, I hurried downstairs and used his washer. Maybe I was pressing my luck, but Hannah seemed pretty level-headed. And given her own forced living circumstances, I thought she'd understand why I'd take advantage of Shax's empty house.

I was on the couch, watching a movie when the door opened.

"How'd it go?" I called.

The door shut a little harder than usual.

I turned to see why, and my jaw dropped. A dark handprint colored Shax's left cheek.

"Holy shit. What happened to you?"

"Hannah said she never wants to see me again."

"What? Why would she say that? Tell me everything that happened."

He took off his jacket and threw it aside, obviously very upset. I listened to the thump of each shoe as he kicked it off just out of sight.

I thought he'd flop on the couch next to me when he marched my way. Instead, he knelt in front of me and put his hands on my stomach.

He leaned forward and set his forehead on my bulge. My little freeloader made a fluttering kick at Shax's head.

"I did what you said," Shax said. "I asked her if we can make a baby together. She said no."

I groaned.

He lifted his head.

"What did you like? I will do it again."

Another groan escaped me.

"The wrong kind of groans, Shax. These are the bad kind."

"There's a bad kind?"

"Yes. There is definitely a bad kind."

"How am I supposed to tell the difference?"

"It's all in the facial expressions, Shax. Pay attention to the looks the girl's giving you. If those don't cue you in, that slap should have."

"I don't like slaps."

I uncurled my legs and patted the cushion next to me.

"Have a seat. We need to talk."

"We are talking," he said even as he moved to sit beside me.

"I never told you to ask her to make a baby with you. Of course, she's going to slap you. You can't just go asking someone that. It's something you lead up to."

"I did. I told her I would show her the difference between sex and conversation."

I groaned again.

"You know that's not how that pickup line went. You can't shortcut these things."

He made an impatient, frustrated sound, and I felt truly awful for him. He'd be lucky if Hannah talked to him ever again.

I leaned over and wrapped my arms around him. Laying my head on his chest, I hugged him close.

"I'm sorry she slapped you. I'm sorry that things aren't working out the way you wanted."

He reached around me, his hands stroking down my back.

"There are so many rules," he said, his voice still carrying his frustration. "Do not say desperate things. Do not ask to see pussy or boobs. Why can I not just say what I want?"

"You do know that's only two rules, right?"

He rested his head on top of mine.

"I like spending time with you. You do not get mad at

me." His hands continued to move up and down my back. It felt so relaxing.

"I bet Hannah wouldn't get mad at you if she spent a little time getting to know you."

Shax snorted. "She does not want to know me. She wants things, like you said."

I cringed a little. I shouldn't have planted that seed in his head.

"I'm sure that's not true. Let's give Hannah some time—a lot of time—and you can try again."

Shax's fingers found that spot on my lower back from earlier, and I melted against him.

"That feels so good."

"Tell me more about what women like in men."

"Well, attention is good. Women like to know they are important to a guy. And, things that are easy to give. Spending time with someone, doing something you both enjoy. That's even better."

"I enjoy giving foot rubs and back rubs," he said. His hands proved it by working their way up my back.

"And females definitely enjoy receiving them."

"So, this is quality time."

"Yep. This would count. If you gave Hannah back rubs like this, she'd be begging you to be her baby-daddy in no time."

He made a rumbling noise in his chest as if he liked that idea.

"What else can I rub for quality time?" he asked.

"Anything really. Just ask a girl what she wants to be rubbed. I'm sure she'll have plenty of ideas if you don't."

I was going to make some woman the happiest girl on the planet with that last little bit of advice.

He started in on my shoulders, and I groaned.

He tilted my head back, so I was looking at him.

"Can I rub your boobs?"

I grinned at him.

"You know what? You deserve something nice after that slap. Yes. You can rub my boobs, Shax. Just be really gentle because they're a little tender."

CHAPTER NINE

SHAX'S PUPILS DILATED THE MOMENT I AGREED TO THE BOOB rub and excitement lit his gaze.

I turned on the couch and draped my legs over his lap.

"Hope you don't mind I raided your dresser. I wanted to wash my clothes as long as I was here."

His gaze locked on my chest and the two lumps hidden under the loose material. I wasn't chesty, but he didn't seem to mind. He placed his palm over my breast, feeling the shape of it like he had my belly. Once he had the shape, he gave it a very gentle squeeze.

"Does that hurt?" he asked, not looking at my face at all.

I smiled.

"No. It feels good."

And it did. Like really, really good.

I shut my eyes as his other hand closed over my left breast. His touch was light, a borderline caress that made my nipples pebble.

"I want to see what this is," he said, touching one.

"If you want to look under the shirt, we better take this upstairs where it's——."

Shax lifted me and raced upstairs.

"More private," I finished.

He took me to the bed I'd used and set me down. I reached up and opened the top three buttons of my shirt and parted the sides. The way he stared told me this really was the first time he'd seen boobs. I was glad it was with me.

"Go ahead," I said softly, leaning back.

The expression on Shax's face as he stared was full of awe. When he touched me, it turned to hunger. My face flushed, and I wished that hunger was for me, not just the female form.

His fingers traced each peak before he started rubbing them again. Gentle lift. Firm squeeze. My breathing grew shallow. When he rolled my nipple between his fingers, I knew we needed to stop.

"I think that's enough for now," I said, taking hold of his wrist and removing his hand. "I'm tired and need a nap."

He grunted and stood.

"I will get some food."

"Thank you."

He left the room, and I closed my eyes, trying to ignore my tingling chest and the throbbing between my legs. After changing positions several times, I gave up and slipped my hand into the waistband of the shorts. I circled myself and tried to recall the last time I'd done that. Too long.

"Angel?" The sound of Shax's voice startled a scream from me as my eyes flew open.

He stood in the doorway, watching me with a confused expression.

"What are you doing?" he asked.

"I was checking the baby." As soon as the words were out of my mouth, I regretted them.

"Show me how. I want to check the baby."

I could lie some more, show him what I was doing, and have an amazing time letting him "check the baby" or I could come clean like a mature, sex-deprived adult.

"I don't think that's a good idea. It's very personal."

"Does it hurt?"

"Only when I don't finish."

"I will help."

I groaned and covered my face with an arm.

"Fine. I wasn't checking the baby," I said. "I was masturbating."

Silence.

I waited an extra few seconds before I lifted my arm to see if he was still there. He was. The expression on his face said it all.

"Teach me." The husky words sent a shiver through me.

"I'm not so sure I should."

"Do women like men who can help them masturbate?"

"I'm not really sure it's masturbating if a girl gets help, but sure. Women like it."

He stalked toward the bed and reached out for the string tying the shorts. My heart raced as he untied the bow and eased the shorts down. I felt the heat of his fingers as they skimmed over my skin and held my breath, waiting for his first glimpse. He didn't disappoint.

Shax stilled, his gaze locked on the light dusting of hair covering my mound. The way his pupils dilated further and his hard swallow made me feel like a fucking supermodel.

Instead of reaching for the treasure he'd been waiting for, his hands skimmed down over my legs. I trembled, the anticipation killing me. My breath caught when he paused to rub my feet before removing the shorts completely.

Naked from the waist down, I waited for what he would do next.

He set his hands on my knees. Tearing his gaze from the oh so coveted pussy, he looked up at me. I gave him a small smile. It was all I could manage with my heart thundering in my chest and my need pooling between my legs.

With light pressure, he eased my legs apart and made a soft sound of satisfaction. I could picture how I looked. Unbuttoned shirt with my breasts peeking out. Legs spread wide so he could see everything. And he was seeing all right. His gaze swept over me several times, lingering on my belly before meeting my eyes.

"Teach me."

Heart pounding and cheeks flaming, I reached down and parted my folds. He made a growly sound in the back of his throat that sent a jolt of pleasure through me. I hadn't thought show-and-tell could be so hot.

Closing my eyes, I circled my clit with my finger. Jolts of

pleasure shot through me and my hips jerked as I found my rhythm.

A moment later, he pulled my hand away, replacing my fingers with his. His hand was big and hot and very good at mimicking the motions I'd shown him.

"Yes," I breathed. "Just like that."

Each circle brought me closer to the brink. My legs shook; and I held my breath, reaching for release. When it came, I gasped and arched into his touch.

The feel of his lips on mine was unexpected. He kissed me hard, his tongue thrusting against mine as wave after wave of pleasure coursed through me.

When it was done, I broke the kiss and removed his hand before I went blind.

"That was amazing." I hoped he could hear me. I could barely hear myself over the pounding of my heart.

The bed shifted, and he pulled me close, tucking me against his large frame. Warm, relaxed, and clean, I closed my eyes and enjoyed feeling safe and wanted even though I knew better than to fully believe it. What had happened wasn't because Shax was into me. It was nothing more than the burning curiosity of his kind. At the moment, I didn't care. He'd made me feel amazing. And no matter what false conditions brought it about, I'd enjoy it while it lasted.

Yawning, I snuggled in.

Falling asleep in Shax's arms in post-orgasm bliss was heaven. However, I woke up alone and with a growling stomach.

Tugging on my shorts, I went to look for Shax.

My clothes were neatly folded on the table, along with another box dinner and can of chicken.

"Shax?"

There was no answer.

Knowing he meant the food for me, I got dressed and started cooking. It was enough food to divide into two very healthy portions. I ate my portion and put the other half in the fridge for Shax. However, as dinner time approached, I decided he probably meant for me to eat that, too.

I debated going back to my house after the car lights went on. I didn't really want to sleep on an uncomfortable couch. And Shax said he liked having me at his place, so I knew he wouldn't protest. And, Hannah wasn't talking to him at the moment, so there wasn't really any reason for me to not stay where I was.

Happy with my decision, I went back upstairs and tucked myself in for a good night's sleep.

THE SCENT of bacon had me sitting upright. I was halfway down the stairs before I registered the low murmur of voices.

I hesitated, one foot in the air. Low voice. Shax. High voice. Was that Hannah?

A foolish part of me shriveled up a little that Shax might have gone to Hannah first thing this morning. And I knew better than to feel that way. I wasn't stupid. I paid attention. I knew how the fey worked. Each one wanted a female. Once they set their sights on one, they didn't shake easily. In fact,

I'd yet to see a fey give up without reason. Being married or underage were the only two reasons they accepted as a real rejection. So why had I put any stock in what had happened between Shax and me yesterday when I knew damn well it had been nothing more than natural curiosity? Shax's interest in me was strictly baby and body, not in me as a person.

Frustrated with myself, I turned around to go back upstairs and let the couple have their alone time.

"Angel," Shax called. "Come eat with us."

Tender feelings or not, I knew better than to turn down an invitation to eat. Changing directions yet again, I hopped down the stairs as if I didn't have a care in the world. Because, honestly, I didn't. There was food being served, I was warm, and nothing wanted a bite of me at the moment. That was all that mattered. Romance and happily-ever-afters died with the quakes.

My stomach did a weird spin when I cleared the corner and saw Cassie. With effort, I killed the happy feeling that wanted to bubble up inside me. Nothing had changed. I needed to keep Shax's infatuation with Hannah in mind no matter what he asked me to teach him.

"Good morning," I said.

"Good morning." Shax's gaze swept over me. "Sit. Eat." He turned back to the stove, and Cassie winked at me as she handed him a plate.

I looked at the table and saw a plate loaded with hash browns, bacon, and eggs.

"I don't know where you keep finding this stuff," I said, taking a seat, "but I'm really grateful."

"Kerr found a place with boxes of dehydrated hash browns. Just add water. So, we have a lot of them. The eggs are from Julie. She's been preserving them in her basement anytime the fey come back with some that are still good. She's using some kind of brine that her grandmother used. It keeps the eggs fresh for months, I guess."

"I'm glad you guys still have your supplies," I said. "What you gave me was taken for the common good the day my housemates arrived."

Cassie gave me a guilty look.

"We hid most of our supplies, just in case."

"So did I. Under my bed. One of them found it while I was gone. I got the couch and no rations because I was trying to keep supplies for myself."

"They wouldn't let you eat?" Cassie said in shock.

Shax growled and turned off the stove.

"It's okay. One guy in the house did set aside some food for me, and Shax has been feeding me too. I'm not going hungry."

Cassie reached out to pat his back and came to join me at the table.

"I'm glad you're staying with Shax, now. But, if you're ever hungry, come to my house. We will feed you. Kerr stocked up a crazy amount of supplies to ensure the kids would have enough to eat. He wanted to go out today to get some more, but with all the survivors complaining about low resources, I think it would be dangerous if he were spotted coming in with supplies."

"I think you're right. It's only going to get worse, though, unless the people here start taking care of themselves."

"Human males aren't made to fight the infected like we are," Shax said, finally turning away from the stove. "The females will starve if we do not continue to bring supplies."

Cassie and I shared a glance. Shax's reaction was probably the same thing every fey was thinking. They would do anything to keep the female survivors safe. Females were their future. Even the bitchy ones.

"You will stay here today, Angel," Shax said. "I'll get you more food."

He walked around behind me and leaned in to put his hands on my belly.

"Eat."

I rolled my eyes and dutifully took a bite. Shax didn't leave until my little stowaway kicked him.

"So I take it everything is going well?" Cassie asked as soon as the door closed.

"The baby? Yeah, he's still kicking when fed."

"I meant with Shax learning you were pregnant. How did you keep him from telling the rest of the fey? I haven't heard a whisper of your pregnancy."

"I made a deal with him. He gets to touch the baby whenever he wants in exchange for his silence. And, I also promised to try to answer any pregnancy related questions he has as long as he asks when we're alone. I've got to be honest, though. I don't know a lot. I've told him he should probably be asking you."

"That explains it."

"Explains what?"

"He came over this morning and was asking how long you could go without food before dying?"

I snorted a little.

"That's all my fault. I was tired and hungry and a little dramatic when Shax invited me over with the promise of food then handed me a smashed snack cake. Afterward, I explained about hormones, but I don't think he fully bought it. I hope you let him know I'm not in danger."

She took a bite and considered her plate.

"I don't know if you're in danger. I have no idea what your starting weight was. If there's a scale here, you should weigh yourself so we have a point of reference from now at least. The sad fact is that we're all a little underfed. With the supply situation being what it is, I think it's best to assume that the baby could face danger in the new future. You need to eat. If you begin to look a little chubby, then we'll talk about portion control. Until then, I think we need to treat you like you're starving."

"You won't hear any argument from me," I said. "If you want to feed me until I look like the Doughboy, I'm game."

I continued to consume my breakfast with gusto.

"So, is that why you're here? Shax went to get you because he thought the baby was dying?"

"I know the fey can overreact. So, I brought over some food because I wanted to see you for myself."

"Thank you for this. I'm sorry I had to cut into your food supply."

"Don't worry about it. Kerr assured me it's easily

replaced. And if Shax starts leaving for supplies, you'll have your own stockpile of food in no time."

As soon as we finished eating, we cleaned up the dishes.

"What are your plans for today?" Cassie asked, putting on her coat.

I looked around the house and shrugged.

"I'm not sure. I've been watching movies. But, that's been getting a little boring."

"Why don't you come with me? I'm going to go visit Mya. I'm worried about her. The stress of dealing with all of this tension isn't helping with her headaches."

I grabbed my jacket, willing for an outing, and left with her.

"Are you comfortable staying with Shax?" she asked as we walked.

"Yeah. Like all the fey, Shax is really nice. I just hope I'm not taking advantage of the situation. I know he's having a hard time getting Hannah on board the Shax Express. I don't want to ruin his chances."

"You think he's still interested in her? He seemed pretty attached to you."

"When have you ever known a fey to lose interest in a girl once he's set his sights on her? And he's not interested in me. You saw him and his interest." I lowered my voice. "Every time I turn around, he's staring at my belly."

"He does seem to have a fascination with babies. You should have seen him with Caden that first night. All of the fey were in awe, actually."

A raised voice caught my attention.

"Now what?" Cassie said from beside me.

When we drew closer to Mya's house, we saw a group of people clustered in her front yard. Not as many as the night they'd raided the supply shed but still enough to spell trouble.

They were yelling and demanding to talk to Mya. They wanted supplies. Food. Answers.

A group of five fey stood outside the house, creating a barrier that the humans wouldn't dare try to pass.

"I don't get these people," I said. "They're perfectly capable of going out and getting their own food. We did it before the fey came. Why do they think it's okay just to come here and to demand someone else give food to them? It's not fair to expect the fey to provide for them just because they're here."

One of the men near the back turned and looked at me.

"When was the last time you were outside gathering supplies?" he asked angrily.

He had me. I hadn't gone since Matt found out I was pregnant. Almost since the last commander died.

"I haven't gone outside the wall," Cassie said when I remained silent. "I'm happy to go with you."

The guy immediately blustered.

"No, you need to stay here. We need you doctoring."

"Exactly. We all have roles. If you were a supply runner at Whiteman, you need to be a supply runner here. It's that simple. Matt Davis's rules haven't changed. You all need to pull your weight to keep people fed."

Some of the group started turning toward us, having heard her.

"Maybe now isn't the best time," I said quietly.

Cassie shook her head and started forward. I quickly followed. No one tried to stop us, but they had plenty to say.

"If you get food while you're in there, you better share with the rest of us."

"Tell her we need more fey out there gathering food."

"Why should we go out when the fey are just standing around doing nothing?"

As we passed between two of the fey, I reached out and touched one of them.

"Thank you," I said. "I know you don't just stand around."

He glanced at me, nodded, then continued to stare out at the group of assholes.

When Cassie and I stepped inside, I saw we weren't the only ones to come see Mya. Several of the other original Tolerance residents were there as well. I recognized Eden and the fey with her. But many I did not recognize.

I listened as I took off my jacket.

"Standing around? Do they have eyes?" Mya said. She looked at Drav. "Seriously, I would feel a lot better if you'd just go out there and hit a few of them in the face."

Mya looked worse than the last time I saw her. Her face was pale, and the way she was rubbing her temple let me know she had a headache.

"No, she wouldn't," Julie, said quickly.

"Their anger will only get worse," Drav said. "We do not mind getting more food."

"I'm starting to wish we hadn't burned the vibrators,"

Eden said. "Might have kept the natives busy with something else."

The guy next to her grunted, his lips curving.

"I doubt it would be that easy," Julie said.

"Food is the only thing that will quiet them," a young man said. "The group I took out yesterday was willing enough to check nearby houses, but there wasn't much to find."

"That's Mya's brother," Cassie whispered in my ear.

"I know what you're going to say, Ryan," Mya said. "But, I don't think it's right to ask the fey to go with these ungrateful people so they can safely search further out. The fey who are here keep plenty busy clearing the infected from the trees. With Whiteman vacant and us turning on the lights every night, we're the new beacon for them. The rest of the fey are working around the clock on the new place. Because the wall's made out of cars, which the humans can't move into place, the fey are doing all the heavy lifting during the day. And since the walls aren't finished and offer no protection yet, Matt has the fey pulling guard duty at night."

"We need to rotate them out," Cassie said. "They've been working there too long with little to no sleep."

"I will start a rotation," Drav said.

"And the ones who come back must rest," Mya said, firmly.

Drav grunted.

Even I could tell it was non-committal.

Mya stopped rubbing her head to glare at him.

"If you continue to bring these people rations, they will

only demand more. Then you're right back to where you were before. Working nonstop with not even a smidge of thanks or respect for it. No, the people from Whiteman need to get out there and get their own shit."

"And the rest of us?" Eden asked.

"We do the same. Gather our own supplies. Just don't be obvious about it, or it'll cause riots."

CHAPTER TEN

I STEPPED OUTSIDE AND INHALED THE COOL EVENING AIR. Spending the day at Cassie's after leaving Mya's had been informative and slightly terrifying. I walked away from Cassie's house with a sense of relief that I still had weeks to mentally prepare myself for what was to come.

My concerns about bringing a baby into this world were continually changing. After the quakes, I'd been worried about just keeping it alive. Then I'd worried about what I would do to pull my weight after the baby was born. With a baby clinging to my nipples, I'd be useless. And while all my prior concerns hadn't gone away, since coming to Tolerance, they had faded a little. As Mya had pointed out, the only job for females around the fey was princess-in-a-tower. The fey would keep us safe and fed.

The one concern that had grown a little stronger was what to do to keep busy. Kids liked doing things. When they were tiny, the "eat, sleep, poop, and repeat routine" was enough for them. But what about when they got older?

I passed a fey, and he nodded at me. I smiled back but didn't stop to say hello.

After a day with Cassie, I knew how very misguided that concern had been. I was living in the world's biggest daycare. Anytime I got tired or needed a break, all I had to do was ask a fey to hold the baby. If the other fey were anything like Kerr, whoever I handed the baby to wouldn't let go. The way that man had entertained Caden—and the way Caden had entertained that man—had been endless. Not only was he loving the kid's attention, but other fey were stopping by to play with the baby and Lilly as well. Kids here were treated like mini-celebrities.

"Angel," a voice called from behind me.

I turned and saw Garrett jogging toward me.

"Hey, Garrett. How did the supply run go?"

"Good. I have this for you." He took a small jar of applesauce out of one pocket and a can of green beans out of the other.

"I know it's not much," he said.

"I can't take that." I covered his hands with mine and stepped closer to push them back into his pockets. It was stupid to wave food around out in the open.

"Yes, you can. There's more at the house."

He was stronger, and I gave up trying to get him to put the food away.

"Honestly, it's okay. I just ate at Cassie's house."

He looked down at the jars then back up at me.

"I know," he said.

"You know I ate there?" That sounded a little stalkerish.

"No." He looked around, making sure no one was near, and my stomach did a nervous dip.

"That first night, Carol was sitting in the upstairs hallway, listening to you downstairs. I stayed up to make sure she didn't cause any trouble. She dozed off, and I heard you tossing and turning, so I went to check if you needed a pillow or anything. The blanket was off, and your restlessness had pulled at your shirts just right. I saw. But, don't worry. I covered you up, and Carol stayed upstairs, so she doesn't know."

I couldn't believe it. He knew about the baby.

"I just wanted you to know that I know, and I'm not like the rest. I don't believe that there's such a thing as a useless mouth to feed. We're all important. We need to protect each other. If we don't, we're as good as dead, already."

"Thank you," I said. "For thinking of me and for not saying anything."

"I was a little worried that you knew I knew when you didn't come home last night. I thought you were avoiding coming home because of me."

"I'm actually staying with one of the fey. It's more private, and I get a bed. It's more comfortable.

"And he's treating you well?"

I laughed lightly.

"Have you ever seen a fey not treat a female well?"

"Good point. Can I ask how far you are?"

I knew he wasn't talking about living distance.

"I think just over six months. I've lost track of the date."

"Yeah. Easy to do without a phone reminding you every time you look at it." He firmly pressed the applesauce and green beans into my hands, and I quickly tucked them into my pockets.

"I'm going out again tomorrow. Is there anything I can get for you? You know, supplies for the future?"

He was so sweet. I thought of all the items in Cassie's house. The diapers. The wipes. The formula. The bottles. The list went on and on.

"As much as I would love to start collecting some of that stuff, I don't think it's safe yet. People would want to know why you're wasting your time with that instead of bringing back food. You should have seen the crowd outside of Mya's house today. They're angry, and it's only going to get worse as more people run out of food."

"I can imagine." He shook his head as if disappointed in his fellow man. "If not future items, is there anything I can get for you now?"

"Food will always be welcome," I said. "Cassie told me I need to eat like I'm starving."

"All right," he said. "I'll make sure to bring as much as I can."

His gaze shifted to something over my shoulder.

"He looks pretty upset," he commented.

I followed his gaze and saw Shax stalking toward us. The fey were typically misread because they didn't have the same range of extreme facial expressions we had. But anyone who paid attention could catch on to what they were feeling. And right now, Garrett was absolutely correct. Shax looked angry.

"Yeah, you normally don't see him looking like that," I said.

"Maybe we should get out of his way. Can I walk you to where you're staying?"

"I'm actually staying with him."

"Him?" There was worry in that one word.

"Angel. Why are you outside?" Shax demanded.

"Bad day at work, dear?" I asked.

Shax blinked at me, his angry expression melting to one of confusion.

"If you're okay, I think I'm going to get going," Garrett said.

"Yeah, I'm fine. Thanks for thinking of me."

"Anytime. I'll stop by with some stuff tomorrow."

Shax scowled at me as Garrett walked away.

"What?" I asked. "Seriously, did something happen today?"

Shax scooped me into his arms and started jogging toward our house.

"Infected got your tongue?" I asked playfully, knowing whatever was going on, he wasn't actually mad at me.

"No, I was not bitten. I came home, and you were not there. Why did you leave the house?"

Holy crap. He was mad at me. Well, not mad. I'd seen fey mad. Shax was barely annoyed by comparison.

"I left because I was bored, and Cassie invited me to go visit Mya. Did you know that the wall is more than halfway done at the new place? But Matt is working the fey day and night. Mya said they're sending some people out tomorrow so that those guys can get a break. If they send you, can I stay at your house?"

He opened the door and stepped inside. When he gazed down at me, he looked even more upset.

"Or not," I said. "If you'd rather I go back to—"

"Your place is here," he said firmly, setting me down. "And I am not leaving."

"Are you sure you're the one to decide that? It seems like Mya and Drav kind of, you know, do all the leading," I said as he helped me out of my coat.

"Drav will ask for volunteers. I will not volunteer. Sit. Eat."

I looked at the table and saw an honest to goodness piece of red meat. Unfortunately, it wasn't cooked.

"How about if I just warm this up a bit?" I asked.

He grunted and watched me move around the kitchen. I had no idea what kind of meat it was. Just that it was a huge chunk. Something my mom probably would have called a roast. I tried to slice a few hunks off but couldn't manage since it was still frozen in the middle. I looked at Shax then handed him the knife. Without a word, he cut it up into slices.

"I'm guessing you like yours rare?"

"Yes."

He watched me closely as I browned us some pseudo-steaks.

They were probably going to be as tough as hell, but I

didn't care. I'd chew until my jaw fell off. I hadn't had red meat in ages.

As I worked by the stove, Shax took the can of green beans and jar of applesauce out of my jacket and opened them. When he was done, he set them down kind of hard on the table. I turned off the stove and plated the steaks.

"Okay, talk to me, big guy. You're obviously upset. Is it really because I left the house?"

"You said the baby needs to be a secret. If you go out, my brothers will find out about the baby."

I considered how the fey treated Caden and thought I understood why Shax was upset. He was being prematurely jealous. He wanted to be the only fey with access to the baby.

"I do want to keep the baby a secret until I feel it's safe to tell people. But that doesn't mean I should be a hermit. I still need to get outside and get fresh air. The fresh air and sunlight are good for me. Both keep me healthy. If I'm not healthy, the baby is less likely to be healthy."

Shax frowned for a moment then grunted. Even if my leaving the house increased the risk that he might need to share, he wouldn't try to stop me. He wouldn't do anything to jeopardize the baby.

After that, he seemed to relax a little, and we had a nice, quiet dinner. I tried asking him questions about looking for supplies outside, but he kept telling me I didn't need to worry about it.

"You do not need to know how to find food. I will find it for you."

And I knew that if he lost interest in the baby, there were

over one hundred other fey who would be willing to get supplies for me. I just hoped Shax wouldn't lose interest for a while.

"Who was that man talking to you?" Shax asked as he took my empty plate to the sink.

"Garrett. He's one of the people who was assigned to my house."

Shax made a growling noise.

"Why was he talking to you?"

"He wanted to give me some food. The green beans and the applesauce you opened were from him."

"You do not need Garrett food. I will find you food."

Rather than let him get all worked up and jealous again, I changed the subject.

"Do you want to watch a movie?"

"Yes."

He left the dishes in the sink and grabbed my hand, leading me to the living room like he was in a rush. Grinning at his quirkiness, I settled on the couch and watched him study the selection of movies. After a moment, he grabbed Beauty and the Beast, and I melted a little.

"Have you seen this one before?" I asked as he came to sit beside me.

"Yes. She doesn't listen and stay home."

I snorted a laugh and leaned into him as he put an arm around the back of the couch and set his hand on my belly. His touch, his attention, and the movie chipped away at my common sense not to fall any deeper into my attraction to

Shax. I felt the way my stomach dipped when his thumb made little circles of the past places the baby had kicked.

"You know what? I'm pretty tired and think I should go to bed."

He didn't comment as I stood and went upstairs. I partially closed the bedroom door and listened to the water run in the kitchen. Guilt poked at me for not helping him clean up, but I needed to play it smart. There was no time for a broken heart in a broken world.

"CASSIE TOLD me what's healthy. I will find you the right food. Do not let your mommy eat Garrett food. It might not be healthy for you."

It was a good thing I was a morning person, or his words would have annoyed me. That was a lie. There was no chance of being annoyed with him when his hand was circling my stomach like that. The warm, soothing caress made a full journey around my belly, then paused. His lips pressed to a spot just to the left of my navel, and he started the journey again, dipping low toward my public line. My breath caught.

"Men will talk nice to your mommy. You should not let her listen. You know who is best. Shax is best."

His hand made another circle around, and this time his fingers nearly hit the V of my legs.

I stage-yawned.

"Boy, am I hungry," I said, sitting up and dislodging his

touch. "I could sure go for some Shax food."

Shax's hand immediately went to my belly again.

"Good morning, Angel."

"Morning. What's for breakfast?"

"Oatmeal. It does not taste good, but Cassie says it is healthy."

I grinned at him.

"I've noticed how you guys like eating meat more than all the grains and vegetables. I like meat, too. But Cassie's right. A variety is good for me."

"And good for the baby. I know," Shax said.

I nodded, reminding myself that I should be grateful by his focus on the baby's wellbeing and not hurt by it.

He gave me the room to myself, and I took my time taking a shower. When I got downstairs, there was a bowl of oatmeal waiting on the table. This one had bits of red in it. I inhaled deeply.

"Strawberries and cream? This is perfect. I haven't had this in so long." I sat down and immediately started eating. Shax watched me closely.

"Should I make more?"

"No, this should be good," I said between bites.

Before I scraped the bottom of the bowl, someone knocked on the door. Shax went to answer. Given how big he was, I couldn't see who was there before he slammed the door shut again.

"Who was it?" I asked.

"Angel?" Garrett called from outside.

I quickly stood and tried to move around Shax to open

the door again. He blocked me.

"He ate your food."

"Shax, move," I said, shoving at him with all my might.

He made that adorable frustrated sound, but he moved back a step. I quickly opened the door.

"I'm so sorry, Garrett."

"It's okay," Garrett said. "I just wanted to come by and see if you'd thought of anything that you might want."

"I really meant what I said yesterday. I'm not picky. Any food will be welcome."

Shax made a growling noise behind me, and Garrett's gaze shifted to just over my shoulder. I held onto the door and the frame to block Shax from trying to close Garrett out again. I knew how he felt about Garrett food, but food was food.

"All right. I'll be back later tonight with some stuff then."

"Thanks."

I closed the door and turned on Shax.

"Food is food, Shax. You know people can't afford to be picky. So, what's your deal?"

"He ate your food," Shax said again.

"First of all, no, he didn't. Well, I mean he kind of did, but the other people took it and split it up. He was just there. He was actually pretty nice about saving me some. Second—"

"He should have taken it back from them and gave it to you."

"Second of all," I continued as if he hadn't interrupted, "getting me food now is like replacing what they took."

"Why take it and then offer to replace it? He wants something." Shax's expression was getting more thunderous by the moment. "A deal. You will not be friends with benefits with Garrett."

I held up my hands placatingly.

"It's not like that at all. Garrett knows I'm pregnant. He's just trying to be nice. He doesn't want anything to happen to the baby. Just like you."

That seemed to anger Shax further.

"You do not need Garrett food. I will get you food."

Without grabbing his jacket, he stormed out the door.

I rolled my eyes and went back to my oatmeal. Apparently, I wasn't the only one with mood swings. The fey always seemed so dramatically outrageous when it came to females. It seemed to be worse with babies, and telling Shax that Garrett knew about the pregnancy probably hadn't been the best move.

Shax had been very clear in his desire to stake a claim on the baby. He'd been possessive of my baby bump since the moment he knew what it meant. Now, he would be even more jealous. For both his sake and mine, I really needed to come up with a way to get him back on track with Hannah. As much as I hated the idea of going to her, letting Shax get any more attached to the baby would just cause us both problems.

As soon as I finished my breakfast, I got dressed and went outside. The day was yet again crisp and cool. But sunny, too. It would have been a nice day if it were filled with normal life sounds. Instead of birds and the rumble of engines passing by, I heard the unhappy murmurs of people walking around, giving each other suspicious glances.

Keeping my head down, I made my way toward Hannah and Emily's place. I spotted Emily rushing my direction before I reached the corner.

"You're going the wrong direction," she said. "Come on." She hooked her arm through mine and steered me toward Mya's house.

"What's going on?"

"Thallirin and Merdon are back. They were spotted by the fey on the wall."

I tried to remember those names and couldn't come up with anything.

"And that's a bad thing?"

"With Molev not here, it will be," she said to me. Then, more to herself, she added, "I wonder how many hearts they have."

"Hearts?" I asked, lost in the conversation.

"Do you really not know? The only way to kill a hellhound is to remove its heart and crush it. Something only the fey can do. Thallirin and Merdon did something, I'm not sure what, that caused them to be banished by Molev. To win their way back in, they have to kill twenty hellhounds apiece. Their count's pretty high already. But for a kill to count, they have to crush the heart in front of Molev."

"So they can't crush the hearts yet."

"Right. And, until the hearts are crushed, the hellhounds will try to get them back."

I finally understood. The hellhounds were coming.

CHAPTER ELEVEN

EMILY AND I WEREN'T THE FIRST ONES TO REACH MYA'S house. A good-sized crowd already stood on the lawn. As we joined those standing near the back, I caught sight of two fey walking down the street.

"Molev!" one of them shouted.

Some of the people in front of us started to shout back.

"Turn around and go back where you came from."

"You're not wanted here."

I glanced at Emily, who had a slight crease of worry in her brow. Open hostility toward the fey was new. People normally weren't that stupid.

The door to Drav's house opened, and he stepped out. The shouts quieted to murmured grousing as his angry gaze swept over the crowd gathered in front of his house. When his gaze touched me, I wanted to turn around and go back home. However, more people were arriving, locking Emily and me in place.

I leaned toward Emily.

"Maybe we shouldn't be here."

She shook her head, her focus locked on Drav and the two-approaching fey. I studied them as well.

Like all fey, the two newcomers towered over the average man. Even from this distance, I could see their long dark hair, grey skin, and bulk. Yet, for all their impressive strength and grace, one of the two was limping heavily.

"He looks hurt," I said.

"Merdon was already hurt when he left."

"How long ago was that?"

"Not sure. A week?"

"The fey are supposed to heal fast, aren't they?"

"Yeah. They are." I could hear the worry in her voice.

The fey ignored the remarks yelled at them by the humans and strode forward, parting the haters, to approach Drav. I grinned. The survivors might talk shit, but they knew damn well who was in charge. Drav spoke to the two, but I couldn't hear what he was saying over the grumbles coming from the people nearest the front.

"Let's move closer," Emily said, tugging me through the crowd.

"Two days behind," one of the fey said. "Maybe less."

"You traveled far," Drav said.

"We went further west, looking for more survivors."

One of the fey grunted.

"We do not know when Molev will return," Drav said. I could tell by his change in expression that he was troubled by Molev's continued absence.

The crowd didn't seem to like it either because the shouts started again.

"You can't expect us to stay here."

"You need to get rid of them."

"You're jeopardizing our safety."

"Send them away."

The antipathy was ridiculous. The two fey looked utterly exhausted. One of them more so than the other. Even exhausted, though, both fey could probably kick the complainers' asses.

"Stay and rest," Drav said. "Mya would like to talk to you before the sun sets. Come back then."

The two fey moved away, and the crowd got angrier.

"Mark my words," someone else said above the rest of the shouting. "We'll be dead in two days if those two don't leave."

Someone jostled into me, and I felt a sharp elbow in my side as someone pushed past me.

"Mya and Drav are doing this on purpose."

"Too many mouths to feed."

Others started to push forward as well.

"They want to kill us all."

Where in the hell did these people think they were going? Did they actually believe something good would happen if they started pounding on Drav's door?

"We have to go," I said to Emily.

She nodded but was moved away from me in the next moment. Wrapping my arms around my middle, I kept my head down and wedged my way out of the group.

When I cleared the bodies, I looked back for Emily. She

was moving her way toward the side of the group just as the first person reached the front door. Not wanting to hang around for what would happen next, I pivoted and hurried down the sidewalk.

I wasn't the only one leaving. A few fey turned away from their positions where they'd been watching from the shadows between houses or near trees. My heart went out to them. How had they not given up hope on us yet?

I hadn't made it very far when Drav's roar echoed from behind me. At least, I figured it was him. No other fey had a reason to be mad other than an overprotective fey. I hoped he knocked some sense into the complainers.

A few houses up, I spotted Hannah talking to one of the fey. Whatever the guy was saying to her had her shaking her head vehemently. They exchanged a few more words, and she turned away angrily.

I tried to speed up my pace to get out of there before she noticed me.

"Angel! Wait up," she called. Without any other choice, I slowed down.

"Hi, Hannah," I said when she approached, her pretty dark blonde ringlets bouncing with each step. She looked like one of those porcelain china dolls. Perfect, pretty, and in need of protection. No wonder Shax had a thing for her.

"Did Emily find you?" Hannah asked when she caught up with me.

"Yeah. She should be coming this way any minute." I looked back the way I'd come.

"No. Emily knows I'm covering this side of Tolerance.

She'll try the other side. How did the meeting go? Were there a lot of people?"

"More than there should have been. All wanting to bite the hand that feeds them."

"I'm glad you see it that way, too. We need the fey as much as they need us. Well, the females, anyway. How many hearts did Thallirin and Merdon have?"

"They didn't say. At least, not that we could hear."

She swore softly.

"I should have gone, but I hate crowds." She shuddered lightly and paled. "God, I wish I had something to drink."

She took a calming breath and tucked her hands in her jacket pockets.

"I heard you're staying with Shax."

"Yeah. The people who took over the house I was staying in found my stash of food and got a little mean about it. Shax didn't seem to mind giving up a spare room. I hope that's okay."

"Sure. It's a smart move. I would have done the same if he wouldn't read into it. Especially now. Things are going to get way worse once we have hellhounds howling outside the walls. I'm never going to sleep again." She swallowed hard and looked away for a moment. "Mind if I walk with you?"

"No. I don't mind." I did, though, because I was having a hard time not feeling sorry for Hannah. Like all the rest of us, she had a story. And I had a feeling it wasn't a pretty one.

We walked in silence for a bit before she spoke again.

"I know there aren't many of us humans left, and we need to watch out for each other, but having the people from Whiteman live here is a bad idea. Not only are they going to sour the fey's opinion of us, but these people are going to start fighting. And, between you and me, this idea of Matt's isn't going to help. These people don't need a Tolerance lookalike. They need a Whiteman. Whiteman kept them so worn down they didn't spend their time thinking about their next meal or if they were getting their fair share. They were just happy to be alive. It also highlighted their need for the fey. Creating another place like this will give people the idea that we don't need the fey."

"Only until they need to go outside the wall for supplies," I said. But I wasn't disagreeing with her assessment of the situation. Things would likely get worse before they got better. If they ever got better.

"Hey, can you wait here a second while I go talk to that fey?" Hannah asked, nodding toward a fey watching us.

"Sure." I watched her jog toward him and wished she wasn't so right about there not being anything in Tolerance to keep people busy. If there was, I would have had an excuse to get home instead of standing on the sidewalk as another fey seemingly annoyed Hannah.

She jogged back toward me with a scowl on her face.

"I know one of them did it," she said, clearly frustrated.

"Did what?"

"There was a box full of food on our porch this morning. Unfortunately, Emily and I didn't find it first. One of my other housemates did. I need to find who left it and arrange another way to leave supplies so Emily and I can tuck some away first." She glanced at me and shrugged. "These people aren't rationing. They get food, and they eat it all."

"Maybe they're hungry."

"There were leftovers in the fridge from the last meal. No. They're bored, and they're scared. A dangerous combination for the rest of us."

She was right about that. We were already seeing the results of bored and scared. If Hannah and Emily were right about hellhounds showing up in a few days, the mood of those in Tolerance would take a nosedive.

"Hopefully, Molev returns soon," I said.

"Yeah. Hopefully."

I spotted Shax's house ahead. It felt weird walking with Hannah toward his home.

"How is it living with him?" she asked.

"Fine. He's nice."

"They're all nice. Has he made a pass at you?"

"No." He hadn't. Not really. Everything that had happened between us was because he was trying to learn what Hannah wanted in a man, not because he was interested in me. So, none of it counted. At least not in a way that mattered to Hannah.

"Good," she said. "Is he feeding you?"

I thought of Shax's shit-fit over the food Garrett had given me and chuckled a little.

"He's trying but is a little stubborn about what I'm allowed to eat. I think he went out today to find some more supplies."

"During the day?"

I shrugged. He had done it the day before. I didn't understand why she seemed so surprised.

"That's what I love about him. He's got balls. I hope no one catches him coming back in with the goods. It'd be a shame if he had to give it all away before he even reaches his house."

I stayed quiet, not sure what to say to that.

"Well, tell Shax I'm looking for him," she said.

I'd known the slap had been a shock reaction. Hell, if he'd asked to knock me up like he had Hannah, I probably would have wanted to deck him, too. Yet, despite her use of the L-word, a protective part of me needed to be sure that her need to talk to him wasn't just about the supply box she found.

"He gave me the impression you were mad at him and not speaking," I said.

She waved her hand dismissively.

"It was nothing. He said some stuff I wasn't ready to hear. But, after I cooled down, I realized he hadn't said anything I hadn't already known. I just needed to get used to the idea."

I swallowed the bitterness that welled up inside of me.

"I'm glad you two are okay, then," I said.

"Me too," Hannah said. She waved and kept going as I turned up the front walk.

The house was quiet when I opened the door. Grateful, I closed my eyes for a moment and let myself absorb what had just happened. Hellhounds were coming, and I'd likely just screwed myself out of a place to live.

"Fucking brilliant, Angel," I said with a sigh.

After hanging up my jacket, I went upstairs and spent time in the nursery Shax had set up. It had everything. The crib. The changing table. Baby supplies. All the stuff that I would have asked Garrett for if I wasn't so afraid of everyone finding out.

I wondered if Shax would let me borrow all of this until he knocked up Hannah with a baby of his own. I thought of them together and cringed. Hannah had no idea how lucky she was.

Feeling a little depressed for myself, I went downstairs and turned on a movie.

I was safe. I was fed. I should have been happy. Why couldn't what I had be enough while I had it?

When the door opened hours later, I eagerly got up from the couch and went toward the kitchen.

Shax smiled when he saw me and stepped aside to let two other fey in. Each carried a large box filled with supplies.

"Did you just get back?" I asked.

"Yes."

"Any trouble?"

He looked at me, tilting his head. "What do you mean?"

"Nothing."

"Are you hungry?" he asked.

The men set the boxes on the table and turned to leave.

"Thank you," I called. When the door closed, I smiled at Shax. "Yeah, I could eat." I'd eaten some of the leftover meat in the fridge for lunch but had wanted to wait for him before eating again. I was glad I did. He took out several cans of food, showing me what they'd brought back. Frozen meats.

Boxed stuff, including a cake mix. And more baby stuff too. Jars of pureed baby food and cans of formula.

"How did you know to get all this stuff?" I asked.

"Caden has all of this, and he is a baby."

"You must have spent a lot of time with him."

"Yes. Until you came."

His gaze fell to my belly.

"You should eat," he said.

I knew he was thinking of feeling the baby's kicks. I didn't mind. And, I would keep telling myself that until it was true.

He opened the other box and smiled at me.

"I found something for you, too," he said.

Excitement warmed my middle.

"Really?"

He nodded, and I moved closer to peek inside the box. There was a stack of books. I couldn't tell what they were so I lifted them out. Every single one had some kind of hunky guy on the cover. Romance novels? He actually thought of me and not the baby. I grinned and hugged him hard.

"This is perfect."

"Now you do not have to leave the house because you are bored." His hands molded to my stomach. "You will be safe."

My heart fell a little. The books weren't for me. Not really. They were to keep me inside, and the baby secret, so Shax could have the baby to himself.

"I think I'm going to go lay down for a bit," I said, withdrawing.

He caught my hand.

"Wait."

He reached out, his fingers trailing my cheek in a soft caress.

"I want to teach and learn some more. I want to kiss. I want to know I'm good."

The way his eyes held mine melted my insides. Whatever his reasons, I was too weak-willed to say no.

I nodded, and he tugged me closer. The possessive way he held me and the low rumble in his chest made my heart hammer. His gaze dipped to my lips.

Everything was saying that this wasn't a practice kiss but a kiss because he wanted me. I let myself fall into the illusion and tilted my head up to meet him.

The first touch of his mouth was soft and gentle, coaxing me to trust and to give. I sighed against his lips, and he deepened the kiss. His tongue swiped against mine, sending a shiver through me. I gripped his arms and kissed him back with all the feelings I'd been trying to suppress. He made a growling noise, and I groaned.

The next thing I knew, his hands were cupping my ass cheeks and he lifted me off the ground, grinding his rock-hard erection against my pelvis. A fire ignited in my belly, and little shocks of need tingled through my core.

I wrapped my legs around his hips and pressed against him. His hands flexed on my ass, and he kissed me with the desperation of a man going under. He took a step toward the stairs, and my heart started to hammer, knocking against my ribs.

I knew what going upstairs meant, and I wanted whatever Shax would willingly give. No, I needed it.

He stopped walking. I kissed him harder, desperate for him to keep going.

"Angel?"

The sound of Garrett's voice shocked me out of the moment, and I broke the kiss, panting heavily.

Shax growled, his grip on me tightening.

Garrett knocked on the door again.

"Shax," I whispered. "Put me down. Quick."

"No. You do not need Garrett. You need me."

Those words broke the rest of the spell his kiss had woven around me, and I wiggled to get free.

"Now, Shax."

He growled but released me. I exhaled slowly, trying to steady my pulse, and smoothed my hands over my hair. No matter what I did, I would look flushed when I opened that door.

Shax surprised me by closing his hand over mine when I reached for the knob.

"Tell him to leave." The words spoken next to my ear sent a shiver through me. I wanted to do just that. To turn around and pick up right where Shax and I had left off. But I couldn't. I wouldn't.

Pasting a welcoming smile on my face, I swung the door open.

Garrett stood on the porch, a small box in his arms. His gaze swept over my face then flicked to Shax who stood behind me.

"Everything okay?" he asked when he met my gaze once more.

"Yeah. Everything is fine. The baby-oven's just overheating, if you know what I mean. It's a nice change from being cold all the time."

"I bet. I found some things I thought you'd like." He shifted the box toward me. As I reached for it, I noticed someone coming down the sidewalk. It was hard not to with the last golden rays of the sun shimmering off her perfectly bouncing curls.

I looked down at the box, before she caught me staring, and saw what Garrett had found. A green pacifier and a baby blanket were tucked between a glass bottle of syrup and some canned goods.

"Syrup and sauerkraut," he said. "I wasn't sure if you were leaning toward sweet or salty."

I smiled widely.

"Thank you, Garrett. That's very kind."

"It's no problem," he said as Hannah came walking up behind him.

"Hey, guys." She leaned forward to look in the box. "Oh, supplies. You better get that inside before someone notices." Her gaze shifted to Shax.

"Just the guy I was looking for. Do you have a few minutes you can spare? In private?"

Garrett's brows rose a little as he met my gaze.

"If you haven't eaten yet, would you like to come to the house for dinner?"

I could have hugged him if my arms weren't full.

"Thanks. I'd like that. Let me just get my jacket."

I turned and almost crashed into a scowling Shax.

CHAPTER TWELVE

SHAX MOVED TO GRAB MY ARM.

"Don't," I said softly.

I sidestepped him, set the box on the table, and grabbed my jacket. It was hard to know what to think or feel after being pinned to the wall by him. I knew Shax wanted Hannah. He had never misled me. Yet, the situation I found myself in still sucked. Why did I want a guy who wanted another girl? The world had enough stuff in it that didn't make sense. I didn't need to add to it.

When I turned around, Hannah was in the kitchen, watching me. I pasted on my best Angel smile.

"You two have fun," I said, slipping on my jacket. "And don't worry. I'll find somewhere else to crash tonight."

Hannah turned a light shade of pink even as she gave me a grateful smile.

I hurried outside before I said anything that would embarrass all of us.

Garrett closed the door behind me.

"Was that awkward for you? Because, it sure felt awkward to me," he said as we started down the sidewalk.

"Yeah, it was." It sucked that Garrett had noticed it. I had rather hoped to keep my demon crush a secret.

Garrett snorted.

"That guy has been chasing after Hannah since they first showed up in Whiteman. I never thought I'd see the day where she would say yes."

In the distance, the first of the car lights illuminated the twilight.

"I didn't realize how late it was," I said, changing the subject. "Did you just get back from the supply run?"

"Just before dusk. We pushed it, staying out as late as we could so we could travel beyond what'd already been picked over. Mya's brother knows what he's doing, and the extra distance was worth it. We found some great stuff."

"Good. I hope that makes everyone happy for a while."

"Don't count on it. Not many of the people who went out were willing to take the chance and go that additional distance with Ryan. So, there was just a small group of us who hit the jackpot. That meant a better haul for everyone involved, though. The people who didn't take the risk will be kicking themselves in the morning. What I gave you was only a quarter of my take." He gave me a sheepish look. "I kept the rest at the house so no one would complain."

"I don't see how they'd dare since you're the one going out and risking everything while they sit on their butts. And, you didn't need to give me any of what you found, either, Garrett. I don't want to cause trouble for you."

He shrugged lightly. "Don't worry. They could have gone out with me if they wanted more food than I'm willing to share with them."

The house was quiet and dark when we reached it. Inside, Garrett turned on the entry light and took my jacket for me.

"Where is everyone?"

"Not sure. They were gone when I got back."

He gestured toward the box on the table.

"What would you like for dinner?"

I looked through what he had and found a can of ravioli. A meal in a can seemed a safe option for not using up more of his supplies than necessary.

"I haven't had this in years."

He smiled and took a can before moving the box to the counter. While I unpacked and put their supplies in the cupboards, he started heating our dinner on the stove.

"What's it like out there beyond the wall, now?" I asked. "It's weird in here not being able to see anything. Are the infected really getting smarter?"

"It's hard to say if they are getting smarter or just evolving into whatever they are. There's a definite difference between the infected that are just turned and ones who have been turned for a while. It's not like the older ones can talk or anything, but there's a certain level of thought that's going on that can creep a person out. The way the infected know how to hide and stay quiet. The way they know to wait by the human food supplies. The way they know how to block an escape route. It all revolves around them hunting us. Like it's more instinct rather than true intelligence."

"Sounds terrifying."

"It was at first. But the more I go out there, the easier it gets."

Part of me felt guilty that I wasn't going out and doing my part. But the risk was too high, and I was too much of a liability. I knew that. However, once I wasn't pregnant, I had no excuses. I would need to go outside the wall. The thought of the baby I would leave behind worried me. What if I never came back? Who would take care of him? I thought of Shax and his fascination and Cassie's assurance that all fey found babies interesting.

"That's a pretty serious look," Garrett said.

"Yeah. I have a lot to consider. Right now, I'm so dependent on everyone to take care of me. After I have the baby, though, that will all change. I'll be able to go out and do my part, too. As much as I don't want to be a freeloader, the thought of what I'd be leaving behind terrifies me."

"There's no reason for you to go out for supplies after the baby's born. Not when there are people like me, willing to help. And, like Shax. I've seen the way he watches you. I think he'd do anything for you."

I almost snorted.

"What happens when he hooks up with Hannah? The fey get pretty devoted to the girls they're attached to."

Garrett considered me for a moment.

"What about another fey? I know some of the women here are completely against the idea of pairing up with one of the fey, but you don't seem like you have a strong opinion against them. Not that I'm giving you any kind of relationship advice, but the women who do have fey partners are pretty protected. They don't have to leave the security of Tolerance. Maybe that would be the safest thing for you and the baby."

He was right. And, the thought had crossed my mind. Yet, my heart was already shaking its head no as I watched him remove dinner from the stove and divide it into two bowls.

"I don't think I can. It wouldn't be fair to me, the baby, or the fey."

He nodded and set the bowls on the table while I grabbed us spoons.

"Well, you have my help for as long as you need it. I know my capabilities aren't as impressive as the fey's, but at least you know you're not alone."

I caught his hand, giving it a light squeeze.

"That means more than you know."

He smiled, and I released him to take the first bite of my meal. I savored the flavor of the tomato sauce coated ravioli. It wasn't the food I would have picked before the quakes. But now, it was pretty damn good.

"Anything interesting happen here today?" he asked after he swallowed his first bite of ravioli.

"Yeah, the two fey outcasts returned. Everyone was in a huge uproar."

"I bet. With Molev gone, that means the fey won't destroy the hearts they brought back."

"Yeah. I heard that also means hellhounds are coming."

"Most likely," Garrett said. "There are more fey here, though. We'll be fine."

I remembered the last time the hounds tore through Whiteman and the sheer terror I'd felt, seeing the red glowing eyes. I shivered lightly, and this time, Garrett reached out to give my hand a squeeze.

"I'm sorry I brought it up. You have nothing to worry about here. The wall is thick and well lit. Between that and the fey, the hellhounds won't get in."

I nodded, and he released me.

"Have you thought of names for your baby?" he asked.

"Nothing serious. When I'm hungry, I usually use a food nickname. When I get kicked, I go with ninja. Sometimes I call him freeloader or stowaway."

Garrett laughed.

"I think something more auspicious might be needed."

"Auspicious? Wow. Haven't heard that actually used in a sentence."

He grinned. "Yet, it's true. You carry the promise for humanity's future. That deserves something more fitting than 'freeloader.' No pressure, though."

"Gee, thanks."

He took my empty bowl to the sink and turned around with a king-sized candy bar in his hand.

"Dessert, ma'am?"

My mouth watered at the sight of it.

"Dinner and dessert? This is going to turn me into a spoiled diva."

"I doubt that."

Garrett broke it open and offered me half as he sat.

"Thank you for having dinner with me," he said. "It's nice having a normal conversation that's not filled with resentful undertones."

"Ditto."

I took a bite and groaned.

"So good."

He chuckled, and we consumed our dessert without another word. I'd barely licked the chocolate from my fingertips when the door opened.

Harry stepped in and scowled when he saw me. Carol wasn't far behind.

"Hey, guys," Garrett said.

"You're feeding her our supplies?" Carol demanded, her gaze bouncing from the wrapper still on the table to me.

Garrett picked up the wrapper.

"You went beyond the wall and found this candy bar? I'm sorry, Carol. I didn't realize."

He said it all with complete sincerity, and I struggled not to grin.

"Carol, you should go upstairs," Harry said.

"I have as much right to be down here as the rest of you." She pulled out a chair at the table and sat.

Harry sighed and did the same.

"How did it go out there today?" he asked. "We got a little worried when you didn't come back with the rest of the group."

"It was fine. Mya's brother went out further for supplies, and a few of us tagged along with him."

Carol made a sound of disgust at the mention of Mya's name.

"Makes sense that the fey-lover's brother would know where they're hiding supplies," Carol muttered.

"Hiding? Do you honestly think the fey have a cache just sitting out there somewhere? I searched over a dozen houses today and killed twice as many infected. I showered in freezing water and am wearing a set of clothes I found in a house a mile away. Nothing about today was easy, Carol, and Mya's brother was right there with me through it all. There was no secret cache of supplies."

"Easy," Harry said, holding up his hands. "It's just that we saw some fey coming back with supplies earlier today. When we checked their storage shed, there was nothing."

"Did you ever consider that they might be gathering supplies for themselves, just like you are?" I asked. "Mya was clear about what would happen once the storage shed was raided."

All eyes turned to me. Harry and Carol were visibly less than pleased with my participation in the conversation. Harry opened his mouth to speak first.

"They have a responsibility to—"

"No, they don't. This attitude of entitlement is why the fey aren't helping you."

Carol turned red.

"Bullshit. Mya is why they aren't helping. She spread her

legs to get control of them. Given your well-fed appearance, I'm guessing you're doing the same."

"Enough," Garrett said, slamming his hand down on the table.

"There's food in the cupboard. If you want me to keep going out, you'll show some respect to the people I bring into this house." He leaned toward Carol. "No matter who they are or what they look like."

Her mouth thinned, but she said nothing.

Garrett held out his hand to me.

"Let's go for a walk."

I willingly escaped with him. As we were leaving, the rest of his housemates came up the walk. They nodded to Garrett and glanced at me, lacking the open hostility of the other two.

"Any destination in mind?" he asked when we got to the end of the road. "We should be fine to go back in an hour. After they eat, they usually go to bed."

I gave it a thought. There wasn't really anywhere for me to go. Not with Shax entertaining Hannah. I briefly thought of Cassie but dismissed the idea. I hated the idea of bothering her for a place to sleep when she already had her hands full with kids and stray fey popping in to play with the kids.

"I don't know. I'm a bit homeless at the moment. Maybe we could just wander around for a bit?"

"You can stay with me tonight. I don't mind sharing the bed. After weeks with a sleeping bag on a cot, a full-sized bed seems a bit too big."

"I don't think that'd be a good idea. Every time I'm there, you have to calm everyone down."

"I'm sorry they acted like that," he said quietly as we walked down the street. "They're just scared."

"We all are, but not everyone is acting out like an asshole because of it." I looked up at the stars, marveling that I could still see them with all the light in the sky. A low moan echoed in the night. I'd grown so used to the sound, I barely noticed it anymore.

"Did you really kill two dozen infected today?"

"Probably that many just to get away from Tolerance. The car lights draw them in overnight. It was a little better on the way back. There's someone here with a bow who's a really good shot."

I looked at the walls.

"We're surrounded, then. Trapped in a way."

He reached out and wrapped an arm around my shoulders.

"No. Not trapped. People leave every day. The fey help us."

"Has anyone turned while trying to leave?"

His slow exhale answered for him.

"It's not as bad as it sounds."

"Just be careful, okay?"

He nodded and released me.

"Oh, I forgot to tell you. The radishes are starting to sprout."

"That's great. Mya said something about having the fey

look for more lights. Maybe we can set up some kind of growing lab in the basement."

A distant howl rose. Another joined it. Then another.

"Three," he said. "Guess we know how many hearts those two fey brought back."

I shivered at the sound, and Garrett glanced at me.

"I think you need to pick a spot and stay in for the rest of the night. My bed's open. And not in any weird, implied way."

I smiled.

"Thanks. But I think I'll try Shax's place first."

"You sure?"

I nodded.

"I'll walk with you, then. If he doesn't answer the door, we'll go back to my place. No arguments. You'll have a harder time falling asleep once the hounds get closer."

I knew he was right. We veered toward that end of Tolerance and walked in silence for several long moments.

"I'm sure this will be fine," I said as we approached Shax's house.

"This feels awkward, doesn't it? Or am I the only one who's worried about knocking on the guy's door and interrupting something. I've seen fey mad."

I chuckled.

"Yeah, you might want to stand back."

"How are you so calm about this? I'm more nervous now than I was leaving this morning."

"Shax won't do anything to me because I'm a girl. And Hannah won't do anything because she gets it. We're all stuck living with people we don't necessarily want to live with. Privacy went out the window the moment the world fell to shit. Sure, it'd be nice to be able to have a house to yourself, but it's not practical. She knows that, too."

"I suppose you're right."

Yet, when we reached the sidewalk, Garrett's steps slowed. Mine did too. And my hesitation had nothing to do with fear. I just didn't want to see Shax pinning Hannah to the wall as he had me.

It sucked having nowhere else to go.

Something must have shown on my face because Garrett reached out when we stopped in front of the door. He wrapped his arms around me and pulled me in for a hug.

"I don't think life was ever meant to be easy. But, I don't think it was meant to be this damn hard either," he said softly against my hair.

I nodded against him.

"I—"

The door flew open with a bang, startling us apart.

I looked up at Shax's angry expression as he glared at Garrett. A low growl rumbled in the air.

"Ah…" Garrett said nervously.

Taking a quick sidestep, I positioned myself in front of my friend.

"Sorry for interrupting your night, Shax. But, I was wondering if I could stay here again, after all. Garrett's housemates came home and—"

Shax plucked me off my feet and carried me inside, slamming the door behind him.

"I'll see you tomorrow," Garrett called through the closed panel.

"You didn't have to say yes," I said, noting Shax's still angry expression. I glanced around the room and didn't see Hannah.

"Where is she?" I asked.

He didn't answer. He just marched right up the stairs.

"Seriously, Shax, I don't need to stay. I didn't mean to make you angry."

He continued his stony silence all the way into my bedroom where he plopped me on the bed. He leaned in, and nose-to-nose, he growled softly.

"Your place is here."

"Okay. I'm a little lost. What happened? Did things not go well with Hannah?"

He eased back a few inches.

"I need to know more about being the kind of man a female wants. The kind of man who gets panties to melt."

"I have been teaching you everything I know."

He growled again, his frustration and anger very plain.

"It's not enough."

"Should I leave?"

"No." He reached down and stroked a palm over my belly. "I need you."

I softened a little and leaned toward him. I could imagine how disappointed he was to have Hannah show up and then leave again.

"I'm sorry it didn't go well, Shax." He grunted and stood abruptly.

"I don't want to talk about Hannah anymore."

"All right." I toed off my shoes as he considered me.

The intensity of his gaze made me wonder just what was going through his head.

"Do I kiss well? You never told me."

I tried to smother my grin. These sexy grey devils had so much confidence in so many different ways. Yet, in other ways, they were still insecure. Not that they really let that ever show. But it was there.

"Yes, I did tell you. There's nothing wrong with the way that you kiss."

The answer didn't seem to make him feel better, however. He grew more agitated. I watched him pace back and forth for a moment before he turned to me.

"Kiss me again," he said.

This time I did grin.

"I don't know what kissing me is going to do to help. I don't think you need practice, just a willing partner."

"Yes. I need a female who is willing. Who likes my kisses."

He crossed his arms and looked at me expectantly.

"I'm not sure what more we can do to convince Hannah. Maybe if I go and talk to her?" His semi-relaxed and slightly expectant expression turned thunderous.

He leaned over me again.

"You will stay here, Angel. Do not leave again." He straightened abruptly and left the room.

I sighed and listened to the howls growing louder.

Garrett was right. Life shouldn't be this difficult.

CHAPTER THIRTEEN

Morning light streamed through the window and right into my face. I rolled over with a yawn and burrowed deeper under the covers. It wasn't like there was a reason to get up at a particular time, and last night, it had taken me a long time to fall asleep. Mostly because after Shax had left the room, he'd left the house, and for hours, my mind had dwelled on what he and Hannah might have been doing. At some point, I'd finally passed out.

Laying there in the bright light of a new day, I listened to the house for sounds that Shax might have returned. Everything was quiet. I tried not to think about what the silence meant. Surely, he wouldn't have taken Hannah home and stayed there. Not with all the people at her house. But, where else would he have gone?

An ache grew inside me, and I pushed it away.

"There's no time for love when running for your life. We know this," I said, rubbing my belly and getting out of bed.

Staying under the covers wouldn't help distract my thoughts now that I was awake again. However, getting up didn't help much either. My mind continued to race with possibilities as I used the bathroom and re-braided my hair.

After I was finished washing up and brushing my teeth, I went downstairs and spotted a tinfoil-wrapped plate on the stove. I went over and lifted the top. Hash browns, bacon, and biscuits with sausage and gravy. All of it was still warm.

My stomach rumbled, and some of my worries melted away. Shax couldn't have spent the night with Hannah if he'd been here making me breakfast, right?

While I ate, I tried to distract myself with the baby. It kicked more vigorously now with food consumption, which I took as a good sign. I wondered again what my life would be like when the baby arrived. Not just how I would care for it but how the world around me would be.

The new settlement should be finished by the time the baby arrived and hopefully most of the Whiteman survivors would be gone from here. Did that mean I would have my own place? Did I want my own place? I listened to the silent house and knew I didn't. If Shax managed to hook up with Hannah, maybe I would take Garrett up on his offer. I just knew I didn't want to be alone anymore.

Before I finished eating the last of my food, someone knocked on the door.

"Come in," I called.

The door opened, and Cassie poked her head in.

"Good morning. I'm glad you found the breakfast I left. You were still sleeping, and I didn't want to wake you up."

She let herself in and took her jacket off.

"You brought this? I thought..." I tried to suppress the disappointment I felt.

"After Shax told me what supplies he'd brought back, I figured you might want actual breakfast food."

"When did you talk to Shax?"

"He came by last night. He and Kerr went to relieve a few of the fey at the new place. He asked if I could come over and check on you this morning. I think he's nervous about leaving you alone."

He'd gone to help his friends. I almost started to cry. Instead, I set my fork down and dropped my head into my hands.

"I can't do this anymore," I said.

A chair scraped against the floor.

"What do you mean? What's going on?" Cassie asked.

"Shax."

"Things aren't going well? He seemed okay when I talked to him."

"It's not him. It's me. I can't keep hoping and getting disappointed and then hoping again. It's driving me insane."

I lifted my head and looked at Cassie.

"Shax has always been upfront and honest since the moment I met him," I said. "He wanted help winning Hannah over, so I've been giving him advice. But in the process of giving him advice, I started falling for him. He's great. Amazing. And, I don't want him to be with Hannah."

"Did you tell him this?"

"Hell no. I don't want to encourage him."

"You're confusing me. From what I've seen, Hannah isn't really that into him. I don't think she would mind. So, why wouldn't you want to encourage him if you like him?"

"It's not just Hannah. It's the baby." I could see I was confusing her even more. "He's fascinated with the baby, which is a good thing because it means I get fed well, now. But he's fascinated to the point that I don't think he sees me. If I encouraged him, I know he would say yes because of the baby, not me. Do you know what I mean?"

"The fey are obsessed with babies. However, if I were you, I wouldn't discount their fascination with females."

"But, do you know what Shax asked? He wanted to know if he could have my baby once it was born."

She groaned and shook her head.

"Exactly," I said. "I just want to be liked for me, not because I have a working vagina. Living with Shax is kind of killing me. Yes, he's taking care of me. But how am I supposed to stop liking him when I'm living in his house? And if I don't live here, where the hell would I go?"

"Let's hold off on moving you out, just yet. I think what you need for today is a distraction. I was going to go over to Mya's house and check on her. Do you want to come with me?"

I quickly agreed because anything was better than sitting in the house by myself and thinking of Shax. In less than two minutes, we were out the door and walking down the sidewalk.

"I'm sorry you had to come out so early to check on me. Who's watching the kids if Kerr's gone?"

"Oh, checking in on you is no hardship. I had to check in on Merdon, anyway. He got hurt again on this last hunt, and I was worried he'd reopened the injury on his leg. As for being out early, it's hard to sleep with the hounds baying half the night."

I felt a little guilty I'd fallen asleep without even thinking of the hounds.

"It wasn't hard to find someone to watch the little ones. Right now it's Brog and another fey, under Julie's supervision. All the fey want to watch the kids so badly, but they're still a little clueless without guidance."

"Speaking of fey," I said, looking around the neighborhood. "It seems really quiet this morning." The spaces between houses and beside trees, where the fey usually stood, were empty.

"The fey who came back from helping Matt are sleeping. I saw a few of them trickling in this morning. I have to tell you, they looked shot. They're wearing themselves out to get that wall done."

"Are they closer, now?"

"Very. That's why Shax and Kerr were willing to go. They think they'll finish up tomorrow night."

"That's great news."

We turned the corner and spotted a crowd of people walking ahead of us. Several of them broke away from the main group and went toward a ladder leaned against the wall. Cassie and I slowed and watched the men climb the ladder. When they reached the top, they stopped and looked down at the other side. The volume of the low moans coming from the infected increased.

A woman came jogging from the right, running agilely along the wall. The quiver on her back bouncing lightly. She stopped near the group and lifted the bow in her hand.

"Who is that?" I asked as she drew an arrow and shot.

"Brenna. Eden and Ghua found her family almost two weeks ago."

"She's good," I said.

Cassie nodded, and we watched as the girl continued to draw and shoot. The moans quieted, and one of the men lifted the ladder from the inside and lowered it to the other side. One by one, the men climbed down and disappeared from sight. Brenna waited with her bow ready until the last man reappeared with a handful of arrows, lifted the ladder, and put it back on the inside. With a nod to Brenna, he returned the arrows and climbed back inside the wall.

I couldn't wait to tell Garrett that one of the people protecting the wall and leaving arrow-riddled infected bodies behind was a girl. I wondered if the fey on top of the wall used the same weapon. My gaze swept the length of the wall, but I didn't see a single fey.

"This can't be good," Cassie said softly.

Ahead of us, I saw the rest of the group had continued walking in the same direction we were headed. Mya's place.

Cassie gave me a side glance, and I nodded in agreement. As we neared Mya's house, I once again heard raised voices.

"You think they would get tired of acting like this," I said. Yet, with nothing else to do, I knew they wouldn't.

"You can't keep sending us out like this," one of the crowd yelled.

"With the hellhounds out there, we're going to die," another yelled.

"We need supplies!"

I couldn't believe they were still demanding supplies after just seeing a group leave on a supply run.

"Are you people insane?" Cassie yelled, marching toward the crowd.

I glanced at her in shock and slowly followed.

"Don't you know what's going on in there? Mya is sick. She has gray spots. I know some of you have seen them. I don't know what's causing that to happen, but it's getting worse. Her sickness could be contagious. Yes, I understand that you're hungry. But is complaining about a few hunger pains worth risking the rest of your health? You don't want what she has. She's not looking good."

I stared at Cassie along with the rest of the crowd. We were probably all debating the same thing. Was Mya really that bad? I knew she couldn't be or Cassie wouldn't have suggested I come. She wouldn't have risked the baby, or me, like that. Yet, her delivery was totally convincing.

One by one, people split from the crowd and scurried back home until only a few remained. Cassie let herself into Mya's house, and I stepped in behind her.

Once inside, I could hear laughing interrupted by bouts of gagging.

"That doesn't sound good," Cassie said, stripping off her jacket. I did the same and followed her down the hall where we found Drav in the bathroom with Mya. Mya knelt in front of the toilet, and Drav hovered over her with an anxious expression on his face.

"Drav, why don't you go get Mya a glass of water? When she's done throwing up, she'll be ready to rinse her mouth."

Drav quickly left, and Cassie looked at Mya.

"Laughing and throwing up is a new one," Cassie said.

"Contagious. That's fucking hilarious. Why didn't I think of that?" Mya said.

"I'm glad you enjoyed it. Those people are getting ridiculous."

Mya wiped her mouth with the back of her hand and straightened away from the toilet to flush.

"They were ridiculous the moment they got here," she said.

"Think you're done?" Cassie asked.

"For now. The headache took me by surprise. Kicked my ass right into the bathroom. I tried a little bit of chocolate, but it was so bad that it didn't even work. Instead, I just wasted what I ate."

Cassie patted Mya's back and helped her to her feet. I retreated into the hallway to let Drav in with the cup of water. We all waited as Mya rinsed, spit, and started to brush her teeth. I debated leaving, but what else was there to do? I figured Mya would kick me out if she got tired of the audience.

Drav fidgeted for a moment then walked off toward the kitchen before Mya finished. I heard the back door open and close.

"He's not doing so well, is he?" I asked.

"They don't like when we get sick," Mya said after spitting.

"They don't like things they can't fix," Cassie said.

"Yeah, I've noticed that."

After Mya finished up in the bathroom, we moved to the living room. Out of all the houses I've been in, hers had the most seating. Probably because there were constantly people coming to complain about one thing or another.

"How are things going with Shax?" Mya asked.

I shrugged lightly, and she wrinkled her nose.

"Really? I thought for sure that with a bun in the oven, he'd be all over you."

I looked at Cassie with surprise.

"Sorry. I had to tell her. With the food shortage and Shax's hesitancy to leave you, I knew he needed help getting you supplies."

So, that explained the two guys who were with him the other night.

"Don't worry. I get your reasons for not wanting to tell people," Mya said. "The humans are assholes, and the fey would be completely obsessed with you."

"Shax already is," I admitted. "With my belly, anyway. Every time I eat, he wants to hold me just so he can feel the baby kick. It was kind of nice at first but, now, not so much."

"Getting tired of being pawed at, huh?" Mya asked.

"After being not touched for almost two months, I don't mind the touching. It's the one thing that is still nice. It's just hard having all the touching and no real feelings to go with it."

"None?" Mya asked.

"Oh, Shax is in love with the baby," I said. "I just really want to be liked for me. You know?"

Mya sat away from the couch suddenly and made a small noise between a hiccup and a burp. Cassie immediately grabbed the small, lined garbage can that was tucked to the side. Mya waved it away and took a few deep breaths.

"We have to figure this out, Cassie," Mya said. "I am so tired of throwing up. And the headaches. And the body aches. I'm just so tired of not feeling well."

"Do you really have grey spots?" I asked.

Mya lifted her shirt and showed me several grey patches on her side.

"Cassie and I think I'm turning into one of the fey because of my time in the caves. The fey have these crystals there that are magic." She shook her head. "Not even kidding a little. It's crazy. There's a whole world down there that we didn't know existed. Anyway, I touched one of the crystals, and I think it did something. During my time in the cave, I got really sick. Headaches. A fever. Throwing up. When I came back to the surface, it got better. Now it's starting up again. I don't know why."

"But no fever this time," Cassie said to me. "I honestly do not think she's contagious, or I wouldn't have brought you and the baby over here."

"I'm sorry you're throwing up so much," I said sincerely. "I remember during my first trimester I felt like shit all the time. I was kissing that toilet every damn morning and sometimes in the afternoon."

Cassie suddenly stood.

"I'll be right back."

Without even grabbing her jacket, she raced out the door.

"Think she left the stove on?" Mya asked with a chuckle.

"She did make me breakfast this morning. I don't know where she keeps finding bacon, but I think I might love her."

Mya laughed.

"When the fey put their minds to something, they can find just about anything. Mom's got a ton of eggs. If you start craving bacon and eggs, you now know who to go to."

"Thanks," I said.

She leaned her head back and studied me for a moment.

"So, you like him? Shax?"

"I do. A lot. All of these fey are amazing, and I'm so glad Cassie said yes to letting me come live here. But Shax stands out above the rest. I don't know what it is about him. It's a certain something. An intensity. A softness. It sounds weird and conflicting, but he's got it all."

"You sound like you've got it bad."

I sighed heavily.

"I think I do, and it sucks that it's so complicated. Our lives are complicated enough, without throwing this shit into the mix."

Mya chuckled again.

"Too true. So, what are you going to do?"

"I don't know. I know if I came on to him, he'd probably say yes. But I want to make sure he's saying yes for the right reasons. Because of me. Not because Hannah's not giving in or because I'm pregnant, or worse, because I'm there and convenient."

The back door opened suddenly, and I gave Mya a worried look. She shook her head slightly and turned to look over her shoulder at the fey walking in. Drav was mid-conversation with two others which I recognized from the day before.

"We must destroy the hearts," Thallirin said. "It is too dangerous."

"What's going on?" Mya asked.

"The hounds clawed through half of a car last night," Drav said.

"It would have been the whole car if I hadn't taken the hearts out and led the hounds away for a few hours," Thallirin said.

"You took them out? That's too dangerous. You should have stayed inside," Mya said, scolding the fearsome fey without a flinch.

"It's too much of a risk. They cannot be allowed in here. We would lose all the females, including you." Thallirin gave Drav a pointed look.

"You cannot destroy the hearts without Molev. You know the conditions."

"We can destroy the hearts," Merdon said. "And we both understand they will not count toward our total. We are okay with that."

"I am not," Drav said.

"Neither am I," Mya added. "You guys are working

hard." She looked at Drav. "This is ridiculous. I understand what Molev was trying to do, but why can't they just destroy the hearts and we say it happened. Does Molev not trust us, now?"

"This is not about us." Drav came over and gently ran a hand over Mya's hair. "You do not need to worry about this. You only need to worry about feeling better." He tilted his head and looked at her. "Do you feel better?"

"A little."

"Are you hungry?"

"Not really." He frowned, the worried look coming back into his eyes.

"You need to eat," he said.

Her eyes narrowed slightly.

"Do not start on me. I know I need to eat. I don't feel well."

Drav grunted and glanced at the other two fey.

"Do you want us to find you some new chocolate?" Merdon asked Mya.

"You guys are so sweet. Thank you, but no. I don't think chocolate is cutting it right now. I'd rather you both go and rest. You deserve it."

The front door opened and Cassie came in, her eyes lit with a weird kind of excitement.

"Mya, can I borrow you for a minute in the bathroom?" she asked.

Without waiting for Mya, she made a beeline straight for the bathroom.

Mya frowned and got up. I hesitated, and Mya waved for

me to follow. Drav moved to do the same, but she stopped him.

"I have two girls with me. I will be perfectly fine. No need for you to follow."

The three of us closed ourselves in the bathroom, and Mya looked at me with a small grin.

"The hovering gets a little old."

I could imagine it did.

We both looked at Cassie, wondering what was up. The good doctor shocked the hell out of me by pulling a pregnancy test out from under her shirt.

"Pee on this," she said to Mya.

Mya's face went pale.

"What? Are you serious?"

Cassie nodded.

Mya went silent for several moments before reaching out and taking the package. We both watched her open it with trembling fingers then I turned around. So did Cassie.

"You know this is going to change everything if it comes back positive," Mya said from behind us.

"I know."

My stomach felt a little sick for Mya. A baby in this world was scary. I knew that first hand. Yet, she had Drav. No one would touch Mya.

I listened to Mya pee while Cassie impatiently fidgeted.

"Hurry up," Cassie said.

"Work on your bedside manner," Mya shot back.

Cassie grinned.

"All done," Mya said.

We turned around; and while Mya washed her hands, all three of us stared at the test she'd set on the counter.

"How long are we supposed to wait?" I asked. I hadn't taken a home pregnancy test. I'd gone to the doctor.

"A minute or two," Cassie said.

But even as she spoke, the lines started to appear. Two of them, as plain as day.

"Holy shit," Mya breathed.

"I second that," Cassie said.

"Are you okay?" I asked.

Mya met my gaze.

"I'm kind of freaked out. Okay, a lot freaked out. But in a good way. I'm not afraid. Well, maybe a little but not for the obvious reasons. I don't even know what I'm feeling, honestly."

"I understand," I said. "I think it's pretty normal."

A knock sounded on the bathroom door.

"Mya?" Drav's voice echoed deeply. "Are you okay?"

She went past us and opened the door. They stared at each other for a long moment, and my heart kind of melted.

"I'm pregnant," she said without preamble.

Drav's face went through a multitude of emotions. Confusion. Surprise. Finally, complete elation.

He made a growling noise and picked her up.

"I told you I don't like it when you growl in my face," she said, laughing. He completely ignored her words and carried her down the hall.

Cassie grinned at me.

"I think that's one happy fey."

We walked out to the living room where Drav was hugging Mya tightly and pacing around with her like he couldn't put her down. He looked at Thallirin and Merdon.

"She is pregnant," he said forcefully. "We made a baby."

The two fey made a similar growling noise, which I took as some kind of manly satisfaction, and left.

I chuckled and took that as my cue, too.

"I think I'm going to walk back home," I said to Cassie.

"I think I'm going to stay a few minutes just in case Drav has any questions once the excitement wears off."

I glanced at the happy couple. Mya was grinning at Drav as he continued to hug and kiss her.

"I have a feeling that may take a while."

CHAPTER FOURTEEN

I PUT THE BOOK DOWN WITH A SIGH. DISTRACTING MYSELF with someone else's fictional woes wasn't working anymore. After reading for hours, I was too restless to keep trying. It was too quiet in the house, and there was too much noise in my head. My thoughts kept going back to the same thing. Shax wanted Hannah. Why not me? Why wasn't I important enough? Why was everything about the baby?

I tossed the book aside and went to look out the window again. It was easy to see in the pre-dusk light that news about Mya's pregnancy was spreading. Fey walked past in small groups, talking. That on its own didn't make me think they were talking about Mya. It was the big belly gestures that tipped me off.

Other than the excited fey, I didn't see many people out and about. Since Cassie scared them away with Mya's sickness, I wasn't too surprised. But I knew it wouldn't stay that way for long. Not with the sun setting.

Turning away from the window, I went to the kitchen. I'd already fixed myself something simple for lunch and knew I needed to do the same for dinner. Nothing looked that appetizing, though, which made me feel guilty. I had food. All of it should have looked appetizing, no matter what crap was going on in my head.

A knock on the door distracted me from my thoughts, and I closed the fridge to answer it. Garrett stood outside with a box in his arms.

"Interested in some food?" he asked.

"Always." I opened the door wider so he could come in.

"I saw Shax heading out this morning with the other fey, headed for Tenacity. I thought maybe you'd want some company tonight."

"Tenacity?"

"Yep. That's what the current residents are calling it."

"I guess it fits. Kind of cool. And, yes, I wouldn't mind the company at all. I didn't realize how quiet it was around here."

He smiled and put the box of food on the table.

"Isn't Carol going to be upset that you brought more stuff to me?"

"Nah. Harry and Carol saw what I was bringing over." Garrett took the lid off the box, and I looked down at a mix of baby supplies.

"Um…"

"Don't worry, I heard the news about Mya on my way in and played it off like this is for Mya."

"Thank you."

"No problem. There's some people food in there, too. I hid it under the formula."

"I'm surprised someone didn't ask for that. Milk isn't easy to come by anymore."

"Given what I left them, I think they know not to ask for more. So, what are you hungry for?"

I picked a just-add-meat boxed dinner.

"This sounds good. And we have some meat in the freezer to go with it."

While he started dinner, I sat at the table and quizzed him about the world outside.

"Is it still hard to leave here?"

"Not too bad."

"I saw a girl on the wall this morning. She's the one with the bow and arrow."

"A girl? That's cool."

"Yeah. Cassie said her name's Brenna. I haven't met her yet, but she looked pretty badass up there, shooting off arrow after arrow."

"I bet."

"So what did you hear about Tenacity?" I asked.

"Not much. Just that the fey were going there to relieve some of the other fey who've been working nonstop. I heard they're close to finishing the wall."

"Yeah, that's what Mya said, too. I don't think it's close enough, though. People were out in front of Mya's house again today, protesting. I don't know why they think the fey should get them food when they're not willing to go out for themselves. Or why they think the fey aren't entitled to some of the food that they bring back in."

"The mood is definitely shifting. I usually give out a can or two when I come back in to keep the peace."

"I wonder how long that'll work," I said.

"Who knows."

"I heard something interesting today," I said. "Besides the whole Mya's pregnant thing."

"Oh?"

"The hellhounds almost got through the wall last night. One of those two fey who had the hearts led the hounds away for a few hours. That's the only thing that kept the death-dogs from getting in."

Garrett turned to look at me.

"Are you serious?"

I nodded.

"Shit."

"Yeah. This wall isn't as safe as we'd like it to be."

"I don't understand how they could get that close to it."

I shrugged. "The lights cast upward. Maybe there were shadows on the ground that were enough for them to move closer."

"Maybe. I hope the fey take that into account and aim more lights toward the ground."

I hoped so, too.

"What do you think about this Mya pregnancy thing?" he asked.

"Not sure what you mean."

"Well, it seems like that's all the fey are talking about.

They're excited. Not a single resentful expression from the lot of them."

"And?"

"And maybe you telling them that you're pregnant would be a good thing."

"Ah. I think it might be safer to wait until the survivors are gone."

He turned off the stove, and I set the table.

"I haven't had a meal like this in a long time," he said. "I hope Tenacity is set up as nice as Tolerance. I like living in a house."

"Why leave?" I asked. "You're not like the rest of the Whiteman survivors. I think Mya and Drav would want you here."

He smiled and carried the pot to the table.

"What about you?" he asked. "What are you going to do once the troublemakers are gone? Once things are quiet again?"

"I'm not sure. Probably start getting ready for the baby, I guess." After pouring us both a glass of milk, I sat and held up my plate.

"I do want to help with that if you'll let me," he said as he served me.

"I could use all the help I can get." I played with the food on my plate and debated how much I should tell him. I decided to be honest so he'd know why I wanted him to stay.

"I might need to take you up on your offer, too, depending on how things work out here."

"You think Shax is having some luck with Hannah, then?" Garrett asked, already knowing to what I referred.

"It's a little too early to tell."

"If Drav and Mya don't mind me staying, I'll ask for my own house if possible. And you're welcome to live with me if you'd like."

"Thank you. Hopefully, after this baby is born, I'll be a little more useful."

"You're already useful. You're ensuring the continuation of our race."

Even Garrett was putting me in a baby maker role.

"Yeah. Sure."

The rest of the meal passed with little conversation. Garrett seemed to sense I wanted to be alone because, as soon as the dishes were finished, he said goodbye.

I closed the door behind him and looked at the dark, empty house. Instead of going back to the couch to read, I went upstairs, not bothering to turn on the lights.

At Whiteman, I'd been so worried about just making it through one day to the next without dying I hadn't had time to think of anything else. Like what I wanted for a future. The problem with my future was that I had no idea what was even possible in this world anymore. Was there more than a walking womb as an option? It wasn't like going to school would happen. What did that leave me?

I stepped into my room and paused in the doorway to turn on the light.

A scream ripped from me at the sight of Shax sitting on

my bed. He had his head bowed, and his forearms rested on his thighs.

"Geez, Shax! I thought you were an infected for a second there." He didn't look up when I stepped further into the room. "Cassie said you weren't supposed to be home tonight. Is everything okay?"

He lifted his head and looked at me. His expression was hard to read.

"I couldn't stay away. You said not to sound desperate. I haven't been. I've kept in what I'm feeling, and it's not working. What am I doing wrong?"

There was no desperation in his tone now, only extreme frustration.

"You're not doing anything wrong, Shax. You're perfect just the way you are."

He stood with a growl.

"Just the way I am is not enough." He stepped toward me. "I need more."

"It would help if I knew what happened," I said. "Did you go and see Hannah?"

"No, I came home to you, Angel. And I found you having dinner with Garrett. Eating Garrett food. And making promises to live with him. You do not belong to Garrett."

"I don't belong to anyone, Shax."

"I want you to belong to me, Angel." He reached out and placed his hands on my belly. I gently removed his hands and stepped back.

"No," I said. "You want a baby, and you think mine is your only chance. But it's not. Did you hear Mya's news?

She's pregnant. That's proof you can have your own baby now. You don't need to settle for mine."

He scowled and leaned in, a low rumble echoed from his chest. It was the first time in all of our dealings that I felt a little nervous.

I backed up a step, and he stalked closer.

"I want your baby, and I want you."

He backed me toward the door.

"I want to touch you. I want to taste you."

I swallowed hard.

"I want you against the wall."

"I don't think this is a good idea," I said.

He reached out and wrapped his hands around my upper arms.

"Then stop thinking."

I retreated one more step, and my back touched the wall beside the door. A slow smile curved his lips, and he leaned in. My heart started to beat rapidly, and the fire I'd been trying to ignore since he said he came home for me burned out of control.

"You're going to hurt me," I whispered.

He paused, his lips an inch from mine.

"Never. I will protect you from everything."

Against all common sense, I tipped my head up to him. Another rumble vibrated through his chest, and his mouth crashed against mine in a kiss so hungry it stole my breath, my focus, and my world.

I wrapped my arms around his neck and pressed myself closer, needing the contact. His hands drifted down my arms and cupped my ass. In the next moment, he got his wish as he lifted me up and pinned me against the wall. Heat flooded me. I hooked my legs around his waist, and he arched against my sweet spot. The thick press of his erection sent a shudder of pleasure through me, and I made a small sound. He growled in return and shifted his hold.

I barely registered that we'd left the wall. He was doing things with his hips, rubbing himself against me in a way that sent wave after wave of pleasure coursing through me. My hands moved from his shoulders to his head for better leverage as I deepened the kiss and ground against him.

He bent forward, arching over me. It wasn't until my back touched the mattress that I understood. He broke the kiss and looked down at me. His pupils were dilated to the point they looked like normal circles.

He reached down and tugged the bottom of my shirt up. Taking the hint, I lifted my arms so he could remove it then reached back to ditch the bra. The sound of satisfaction he made at the sight of my bare breasts made me grin.

His hand covered one mound as he bent forward to claim the other with his mouth. The heat of his tongue and firm suction paired with the gentle kneading of the other breast pulled me under, and I floated in a haze of bliss. My hands drifted to his head, and I toyed with the tips of his pointed ears. He growled, nipped my nipple, and thrust against me.

"More," I panted. He did it again and again, rocking against my clit and driving my need for release higher.

He switched sides, his teeth scraping against the other

nipple. Between that and the grinding, I found my release and cried out.

He growled loudly and arched into me harder, the speed increasing. Waves of pleasure continued to wash over me, and I tugged his head up to kiss him hard. He came with a moan, jerking against me. I shuddered and held on for dear life as I rode out the bliss.

With a final jerk, he stilled then rolled us to our sides. I lay still, not having the energy to do more than gasp for air.

His hands trailed over my exposed torso.

"Did I hurt you?" he asked.

"No. You were amazing."

He grunted and rolled me to my other side so he could pull me closer. Being spooned by Shax changed everything. It felt so right. Like I'd found where I was meant to be. My future.

His lips trailed gentle kisses down the back of my neck, and he wrapped his arms around my waist. Tiny aftershocks coursed through me.

If that was what happened with clothes on and no penetration, I couldn't fathom what would happen when we did the real deed. Smiling to myself, I closed my eyes.

"Sleep, my Angel."

I woke alone, the other side of the bed cold. I tried not to let it break my heart, but it did. It was barely dawn, and Shax was already gone. I'd been in this situation before and knew what it meant.

Laying there, I let clarity paint the real picture of what had happened the night before. I'd gotten carried away with my pregnant lady hormones and read more into the situation than what there was. He'd wanted to learn more. To be the kind of man Hannah would want. Last night had been about learning for him. He'd definitely discovered some new tricks. My nipples still tingled from the memory. And he'd experienced his first orgasm with a girl because of me. Trying to put emotions into what was nothing more than a fun session of casual sex to him wouldn't do either of us any good.

Swallowing hard, I listened to the bird outside my window and tried to pull myself together. I couldn't be mad at Shax for last night. Not when I knew darn well where his interests lie. This was on me. I needed to—

My eyes widened, and I rushed out of bed and threw back the curtains to look outside. My gaze swept over the trees, trying to spot the elusive little creature making all the noise. Instead of a bird, I saw a fey standing near a tree in our backyard. He must have been looking for the bird, too, but the movement of the curtains had drawn his attention to me.

It only took half a second to figure out why he was staring.

I gave a half-hearted wave and mouthed the word "sorry" before closing the curtains and looking for a shirt.

"Well, I'm pretty sure he didn't notice you," I said,

patting my belly. What was one more educated fey in Tolerance?

After fixing my clothes, I went downstairs to find some breakfast. Hearing the bird had changed my outlook. Yes, it sucked that I'd fallen a little further for Shax. But, birds were back. That had to mean something good.

Someone knocked on the door while I was taking a box of cereal out of the cupboard. I thought of the fey I'd flashed and wanted to groan. The fey had so little in their lives already. I hated the idea of opening the door and having to tell him what he'd seen wasn't an invitation. Putting the box back, I squared my shoulders and went to answer the door.

"Hey, Angel," Garrett said.

I scanned the yard behind him and breathed a sigh of relief when I saw it was empty.

"Expecting someone else?" he asked, amused.

"Kind of hoping I won't be," I said, pulling him inside and closing the door. "I accidentally flashed a fey this morning and was worried it was him knocking."

"There's got to be a story behind that."

"I heard a bird."

"I did, too. Couldn't see it, though."

He followed me to the kitchen.

"Me neither. That's how I got spotted. Looking out the window for it. There was a fey in my backyard. I think he was looking for it, too. What do you think it means?"

"Well, it probably means you shouldn't open the curtains when you're naked."

I leaned against the counter and rolled my eyes at him.

"Ha-ha. You're a comedian this morning. The bird. The animals left just before the quakes, right? What do you think it means that they're back?"

"We heard one. It doesn't mean animals are back."

"But, it does seem like a good sign, right?"

"Perhaps. Animals can sense things we can't. I think, before the quakes, they knew some kind of natural disaster was coming and fled to areas they felt were safer."

"So if a bird is here, it feels this is a safe place now?"

He shrugged. "Or that there's no impending disaster here. Or, maybe, the bird just got lost and happened to land here and took off already. It's impossible to know unless they start talking."

"Don't even say that. The infected and hellhounds are enough to deal with."

He grinned.

"Did you just come here to creep me out?" I asked.

"No. With so many of the fey helping with Tenacity or grabbing some Z's, I decided not to go out and came to see if you wanted to hang out with me today."

As I looked at Garrett's hopeful face, I thought of Shax and what we'd shared the night before. The best way to not think about things I couldn't have was to focus on the things I could.

"What did you have in mind?"

CHAPTER FIFTEEN

GARRETT TUCKED HIS HANDS IN HIS COAT POCKETS AND
continued to smile at me.

"To start, I'd like to feed you breakfast. I feel like I need to
make up for last night. I was tired and not participating in the
dinner conversation like I should have been."

Garrett was obviously a great guy. Why couldn't I feel any
attraction to him?

"I'm not letting you apologize for being tired when it's
because of freeloaders like me. But, yes. I'd love to have
breakfast with someone instead of alone. I have some stuff
here."

"Nope. I have everything we'll need at my house."

I grabbed my jacket and followed him out the door.

"Do you know what I miss?" I said, looking up at the sky.
"The weather report. I hate not knowing if it's going to snow
or rain or what the temperature will even be the next day."

He chuckled.

"I don't think that even ranks in the top ten things of what I miss most."

"Oh? What do you miss?"

"The idea of a vacation. Public transportation. Hell, any transportation that wouldn't end with me swamped with infected. Pizza. Man, I miss Pizza. Entertainment. Any form. Movies. Bowling. Skiing. Baseball games. All of it." He paused for a moment, growing serious, and looked toward the wall. "Most of all, I miss my family."

"I'm sorry, Garrett."

"No, it's okay. It's just part of life now. I know everyone is missing someone."

"That doesn't stop the pain, though. Where did you live?"

"New York. I was here on business, staying at a hotel in Kansas City when everything went down. The Evac was crazy."

"New York is pretty far from here," I said. "You never know. You might still have family out there."

"That's what I tell myself. But I'll never know because that's a distance I'll never be able to cross."

"Never say never," I said. "We heard a bird today, and I never thought we would hear one of those again, either. I think that means change is coming."

"I just hope it's good change."

As we neared the house, I looked at the wall. There wasn't a single fey standing on top of it again today.

"I felt safer when I saw fey walking around. I know it's not very fair that they had to do it all the time, but it sure did give me peace of mind."

Movement at the base of the wall caught my eye. One of the fey was talking to the girl with the bow and arrow. He stood a respectful distance from Brenna, but I could tell Brenna was uncomfortable.

As we drew closer, I realized it was Thallirin, and my heart went out to him. He was so scarred. More so than any other fey. I couldn't imagine that those scars would make winning over any girl easy.

"Budding romance?" Garrett asked, noting the direction of my gaze.

"Based on the body language, I doubt it. At least, not from her point of view."

"Would it sound weird if I said I sometimes wished I was a girl?"

"Yep."

He grinned.

"It'd be nice to have one of the fey looking out for me like they do for you girls."

"Given their general fascination with seeing female genitalia, I think they're all heterosexual. But, you can try hitting on one if you want. Warn me first, though, so I can make some popcorn and enjoy the show."

"The apocalypse made you bloodthirsty."

"Nah," I said. "Raging hormones do that."

He chuckled and shook his head. I liked bantering with Garrett. He was fun, good-looking, and smart. I set my mind to trying to like him more than a friend.

When we reached the house, he opened the door to a

quiet kitchen with a table set for two. The smell of something delicious drifted in the air.

"Where is everyone?"

"I asked for some alone time after all the supply runs."

"And they agreed?"

"They like the supplies, so yeah."

He helped me out of my jacket and pulled out the chair for me. Before I could ask what he'd made, he lifted the lid on the covered plate set in the center of the table, and I saw a stack of homemade waffles.

"No way." I inhaled deeply.

"I found a waffle maker while I was out there, and a surprisingly plentiful quantity of pancake and waffle mix. Dig in."

I did just that. Breakfast was enjoyable and smothered in syrup. After I'd packed in as much as I could, we moved to the living room and watched two movies. It wasn't the usual PG stuff that most houses had. It was a good old-fashioned action adventure with a bit of blood.

"Is it just me or does this seem less intense now?" I asked after the credits rolled.

"I wasn't going to mention it, but yes. What's really happening out there is far more intense than any movie."

I stood and stretched.

"Are you hungry for lunch?" he asked. "I found some hamburger buns in someone's freezer and the ground beef to go with it."

"We better not," I said. "I don't want to push your

roommates too far. And, honestly, I think Junior wants me to take a nap."

"I'll agree to a nap break if you agree to having dinner with me later."

"Deal."

After putting on our jackets and boots, he walked me back to my house. The air felt a little cooler than several hours ago, and I wondered if we were in for a storm. Everything around us felt so hushed, like Tolerance was waiting for one. Which was ridiculous because there weren't any animals around to hush. Then I realized what was missing. No one else was out walking.

"Is it just me or does it seem uncommonly quiet today?"

He looked around.

"I think a lot of the fey went to the new place to try to finish things up today."

"Yeah that explains why they're missing, but where are all the people? They're always walking around in little groups, complaining about shit."

He frowned slightly and scanned the area again.

"Maybe a bigger group went out for supplies today," he said. But I could hear the doubt in his voice. Likely because he was thinking the same thing as me. The survivors were up to no good.

My pace increased as we drew closer to Shax's house. No matter how I tried to distract myself, I hadn't stopped thinking of Shax in some way, and I couldn't help wondering if he was maybe home. I really wanted him to be. I was pathetic.

When we reached the front step, I turned to Garrett.

"Thank you for walking me home and for breakfast and the movies. It was nice just hanging out with someone."

"Anytime. And I was serious about dinner. I'll be back at five, okay?"

"It's a date," I said playfully as I opened the door.

His gaze went from my face to the entry behind me, and the humor vanished from his expression. I followed his gaze, and my mouth dropped open.

The inside of Shax's house was trashed. The entry table was knocked to its side, the contents of its little drawer strewn about. Beyond that, I could see bits of fluff on the floor.

"What the hell?" I said softly.

I moved to enter, but Garrett grabbed my arm.

"I think I should go first," he said.

I nodded and let him step past me. He led the way into the kitchen where I saw cupboards hanging open, all of them empty.

"No," I said, moving forward. I checked the fridge, the pantry, everything. There wasn't a speck of food left. Not even the leftovers.

"Who would do this?" It was obviously people, but who would have balls big enough to take from one of the fey.

"I don't know," Garrett said, continuing to the living room.

The couch was overturned, the cushions and back cut open. More bits of fluff were everywhere from the stuffing being pulled out. Even the TV was knocked over.

"I can understand the supplies, but what's up with

wrecking everything?"

Garrett remained silent, looking at everything with an angry expression. We continued moving through the first floor, finding damage here and there.

"I think they were looking for hidden supplies," he said finally after seeing the towels thrown out of the linen closet.

We went upstairs, and my heart plummeted at the note taped to my door.

"No useless mouths," it read.

Garrett tore it off and balled it up.

"You're not useless," he said.

"But someone thinks I am. They left this on my door." I looked in my room. The mattress was on its side and cut to hell. The bed frame was moved, the dresser drawers tossed around, and the dresser tipped over.

I went to the baby room that Shax had set up. The supplies useful to adults, like the baby formula and wipes, were gone. The diapers and baby toys were still there.

Shax's room was untouched.

"If they went through here, they were very careful about it," Garrett said.

"It's not going to save them," I said. "He'll still want to tear off some heads for this. He put that baby room together before he knew about me. And, he'll be pissed about what they did in my room."

"And that's why we need to clean this up before Shax gets back," Garrett said quietly. "We can't allow two people to start a war between the fey and the humans."

He'd said two people.

"What if this wasn't just Carol and Harry being dicks? What if this is more widespread than that? You saw it out there. No one was walking around. This place is going to shit."

"And we have to do everything we can to stop it from getting any worse."

I sighed heavily, pissed beyond measure but knowing he was right.

"Fine. Let's start downstairs."

We worked together to try to fix what had happened. I re-stuffed the couch and draped the blankets over the cushions, so the worst of the damage was hidden. Then I got out the vacuum to clean up the fuzz I missed. While I did that, Garrett swept some spilled sugar from the kitchen floor.

"Shax isn't an idiot," I said. "He's going to notice the missing food even if he doesn't catch on to the cut-up couch."

"We can take the couch from my place and switch."

"I hate that couch," I said under my breath.

It took us a long while to clean up downstairs before we could move upstairs. My stomach gave a quiet rumble of protest over missing a meal. But, I knew we needed to keep cleaning. I did not want Shax to see the full extent of the damage done to his home.

"This really annoys the hell out of me. I mean I understand Carol is all bitter and everything because she lost her daughter, but like you said, we've all lost someone. You're not acting like that. Neither am I. I think people just use past struggles for an excuse to be assholes in the present. They're making a conscious choice about who they want to be."

I lifted a bit of my mattress from my bedroom floor, a cut-out square with part of a spring attached.

"I mean, look at this. What's the point? This is just pure bitterness. What they don't get is that the bitterness they're directing at me can't hurt me. But it will hurt them. It's already eating away at their insides. Tonight, though, I'll still be sleeping on a nice mattress because Shax probably won't have it any other way. What he's going to want is names."

Garrett looked at me with concern.

"Oh, don't worry. I'm not going to tell Shax, no matter how much it tempts me."

We righted the mattress and the dresser, which helped the room look less ransacked. There wasn't much I could do about the mattress. Garrett fetched the vacuum and went to work in the baby's room while I continued to erase the evidence of what had happened in my room.

The daylight was starting to fade by the time I turned off the vacuum. As I was surveying the room, the baby kicked hard, and I put my hand over my stomach.

"Are you okay?" Garrett asked, having walked in behind me. He looked around the room and went to close the closet door.

"Yeah, that one was just a little hard and deep."

"Should we stop?"

"No, I really want to keep doing this. I know this is going to sound weird, but it feels good to do something even if that something is bad."

A roar filled the hallway, making my ears ring. I pivoted to face the door just as Shax charged into the room. His angry gaze swept over me then Garrett.

"Angel is mine," Shax said. "You will not ever go hard and deep with her."

Garrett's face paled, and I busted out laughing.

"I was talking about the baby kicking, Shax."

Shax glanced at me, some of the anger clearing from his expression. I saw the moment his gaze swept over the rest of the room. We hadn't yet covered the mattress with the quilt.

Shax growled. His arm whipped out, and before I knew what was happening, he held Garrett off the ground with one strong hand wrapped around my friend's throat.

"Shax, stop," I said, reaching for his arm. "I swear if you hurt Garrett, you're never going to touch the baby again."

Shax immediately dropped Garrett.

"He stole your food, and now he destroyed your bed. Why do you continue to defend him? Do you love Garrett?" he demanded angrily.

I chose to ignore the last part of his question, knowing his jealousy wasn't from the heart but for the potential threat of losing his access to the baby.

"Garrett didn't do this. The house was trashed when we got here."

Shax tilted his head and looked at me.

"You left the house? With Garrett?"

Knowing he wouldn't let this go, I gave in and answered.

"Yes. And if I hadn't, I would have been here when whoever broke in destroyed the place. What do you think would have happened then?"

Shax's jaw muscle twitched, and he clenched his fists. The low growl that filled the room had Garrett backing away.

Whether for me or just the baby, his fierce protection was endearing. In a world filled with monsters, there was a sexy, grey devil ready to fight for this Angel; and I could do nothing but thank him for that.

I stepped up to Shax and gently cupped his face. The muscles under my fingers twitched and jumped as he stared down at me, but he stopped growling.

"I'm safe, Shax. Because you're letting me stay here. Because you're taking such good care of me." His expression softened, and he reached for me, his hands splaying over my belly where the stowaway still kicked lightly. A soft rumble of satisfaction rolled through Shax, and I watched his pupils dilate slightly.

I decided why he wanted me didn't matter anymore. He wanted me, and I'd hold onto that for as long as I could. But I wouldn't do it blindly. I couldn't solely belong to Shax when he might someday win over Hannah. I couldn't isolate myself like he wanted.

Gently stroking my fingers over his skin, I told him what he needed to hear and understand.

"But I need to be safe when you're not here, too. Garrett was kind and kept me company and helped me clean up. Some of the humans here are assholes. But Garrett isn't one of them. He's a friend, and I need friends."

Shax's expression changed. His pupils narrowed, and the muscles under my fingertips hardened.

"A friend with benefits?" Shax growled.

I grinned.

"I really don't think that's funny," Garrett said quietly.

Shax would have turned to look at Garrett, but I kept my hands on the sexy, grey devil's face.

"Are you jealous?" I asked.

Shax stopped growling and looked away from me.

"Yes."

"You have no reason to be." I moved my hands from his face to his shoulders. Some of the tension left him as he studied me. I didn't know what he was thinking, but whatever it was, it had his mind racing until he looked at Garrett.

"Did Angel teach you kissing?"

Garrett opened his mouth, but I beat him to the answer.

"No, Shax. You're the only one I've taught," I said without a hint of embarrassment.

My stomach took that moment to let out a loud gurgle, drawing Shax's attention. His brow creased with worry and his hands roamed over my belly.

"It's fine," I said. "We just skipped lunch."

Shax's gaze narrowed on Garrett, and Garrett held up his hands.

"Not my fault," Garrett said quickly. "All the food is gone here. But I have some at my house. We can get her what she needs from there."

Shax's focus settled on me again.

"Who took your food?"

"I don't know," I said. "It could have been anyone. All the humans are hungry, and they don't know that I'm pregnant. They just think I am some girl mooching off one of the fey."

"Mooching?"

"It's slang for using someone."

"You are not using me. We have a deal. And that deal now includes no eating Garrett food. I will find what you need."

I struggled to smother my grin as Shax released me to glare at Garrett. I waited for him to say something suitably claim-staking to let Garrett know who Shax thought I belonged to.

"Will you keep Angel safe while I look for food outside the wall?" Shax asked.

"Of course," Garrett said openly relieved.

Shax folded his arms.

"No kissing. No asking to see her boobs. And no touching or tasting her pussy."

"I swear I will keep my hands and lips to myself," Garrett said.

"Your penis, too," Shax said, taking a menacing step toward the man.

Garrett lifted both hands.

"I swear!"

Shax grunted and looked down at me.

"Don't take too long," I said. "It's close to dark, and those hounds will be back."

He lifted one of my hands from his chest and kissed the palm. A shiver stole through me, and his lips curved into a knowing smile.

"Stay in the house," he said softly.

Before I could answer, he was out the door.

"I think I need a clean pair of underwear," Garrett said.

"Nah, you were fine the whole time. Still want to hit on one of them?"

"No way. Not for all the protection in the world."

"Baby."

My stomach rumbled again, and a wave of queasiness washed through me.

"Ungrateful, Sea Monkey," I said, rubbing my stomach. "I think I better go sit in the kitchen. There's mutiny afoot."

However, sitting in the kitchen didn't resolve the queasiness. It just made it worse, and I knew I was getting too hungry.

Garrett fidgeted.

"I would say I could run to the house, but I'm not exactly sure what I'd find there. And I don't want to leave you alone and have Shax come back while I'm gone."

"And you don't want Shax to find out I ate Garrett food," I added.

"Yeah, there is that. But, I'd risk it to get you something to eat before you get sick," he said. "Is there anywhere else we can go?"

"Yeah," I said, standing and grabbing my jacket. "Are you sure you're willing to risk Shax's wrath by leaving the house?"

Garrett put on his jacket and sighed heavily.

"For you and the baby, yes." He opened the door and looked down at me. "I'll keep you safe from the humans, and you can keep me safe from the giant fey who's in love with you. Deal?"

CHAPTER SIXTEEN

"HE'S NOT IN LOVE WITH ME," I SAID, YET AGAIN, AS I knocked on Cassie's door.

"Sure. All the touching and long looks are due to hand and eye seizures."

"I liked you better when you were on team Carol and Harry."

Garrett's chuckle immediately cut off when Kerr yanked open the door.

The big fey didn't look like his normal self. His clothes were rumpled, the skin under his eyes was almost black, and his expression was more stoic than usual.

"Hi, Kerr. Is Cassie around?"

"She's sleeping."

"Oh." I looked away for a moment, debating what to do when my stomach gurgled again. The cramping pain that went with it was not okay. I was used to being fed regularly, and the baby was making it loud and clear that starvation wasn't an option.

I met the fey's gaze.

"People broke into Shax's house and stole all our food. Shax left to get some more, but I don't think I can wait. I'm so hungry I feel sick."

Kerr grunted and opened the door wider. His gaze flicked to Garrett.

"Shax made Garrett promise to keep me safe. Is it okay if Garrett comes in, too?"

Kerr grunted again and stepped out of our way. When he closed the door, I could tell by his slow and measured movements that something was wrong.

"Are you sick, Kerr?"

"Tired. The hounds are keeping the children awake at night."

"I'm so sorry. If you're comfortable with me grabbing a quick snack on my own, you can go back to bed. I promise not to eat too much."

"You'll eat as much as you need," Cassie said, appearing at the end of the hall. "Come on."

"I'm so sorry I woke you."

She gave me a rueful smile then went to Kerr and wrapped her arms around his waist.

"You didn't wake me. I felt Kerr missing even in my sleep. I got up to take over sitting with whichever one of the kids he'd heard. I don't think he's slept since the hounds arrived."

"You need sleep," he said softly, kissing the top of her head.

"So do you, you stubborn man." She met my gaze and smiled tiredly. "What are you hungry for?"

"Anything. I'm not picky."

She led the way into the kitchen and went to the cupboard for a box of cereal while Kerr took out a bowl and spoon for me. I watched them work together and struggled not to feel jealous.

"I'm glad your appetite is increasing," Cassie said. "It's impressive you cleared the house of supplies. We should weigh you again."

"I didn't clear the house." I sat at the table and poured some cereal. "Someone else did."

"Thoroughly," Garrett added, leaning in the doorway to the kitchen.

"And viciously, based on the state of my mattress."

I had to pluck the milk from Cassie's fingers while she stared at me in shock. Cereal for dinner sounded terrific, and I was ready to eat the whole box.

"Someone broke in and took everything?" she asked, sitting beside me.

"Since we don't lock doors, I'm not sure we can call it a break in. But, they took anything they could eat or drink." I took a big bite of cereal and chewed slowly.

"Seriously, I think you just saved my life," I said. "It felt like the baby was trying to eat its way out."

Kerr made a weird noise, and when I looked at him, his eyes were wide and slightly terrified.

"Ah crap," I said at the same time Cassie said, "The baby wasn't really eating her."

Kerr's gaze shifted from Cassie to my belly and back to Cassie. I should have regretted letting the cat out of the bag, but I'd known I wouldn't be able to keep it a secret forever. Plus, it was his hard work that was feeding me at the moment, so I couldn't complain.

"It's why I was worried about her getting enough to eat," Cassie said.

"Are there more pregnant females?" he asked.

"Not that I know of," she said. "Just Mya and Angel."

"And I'd prefer that no one else knows about my baby," I said around a mouthful of cereal. I finished chewing and swallowed quickly. "I don't think it's safe. Someone left a sign on my door. 'No useless mouths.' Can you imagine what people would say if they knew I was pregnant instead of thinking I have blood sugar issues?"

Cassie frowned and glanced at Kerr.

"We need to speak to Mya and Drav about this," she said. "Physical violence will be next."

"Yes," Kerr said. "It is right to hurt the humans responsible."

"That's not what I meant," Cassie said. "We need to address the food shortage before the situation escalates to violence."

Kerr grunted and reached for a jacket by the door.

"I want to come too," I said, eating faster.

"Slow down. We'll all go. Kerr's just going to find someone to watch the kids."

I nodded and chewed like a normal person. Well, a hungry, pregnant normal person.

By the time I finished my cereal, my stomach was happy and the queasiness had subdued. Julie arrived with two fey and Kerr not long afterward.

"That was quick," Cassie said.

"I was on my way over here. Mya sent me. People are back outside her house. Seems word's spread about the baby, and some folks aren't too happy. And, you can imagine Drav's reaction."

Cassie shook her head.

"They aren't seeing the long-term picture."

"Maybe they are, but it's just not the same version as yours," Julie said. "Fear and grief can cloud how people think. And given what we've all been through, what we're all still going through, I think we're going to see a lot of irrational behavior. It doesn't mean we should give up on them, though."

Garrett and I shared a look.

"You're right," Cassie said. "The kids are already sleeping. We put them down early, hoping that they wouldn't hear the hounds tonight. We soundproofed their rooms as best we could, too."

"We'll keep the kids safe. Go calm down Drav before he kicks everyone out of Tolerance."

I wasn't so sure the news we had would have the desired effect.

Outside, the wind had picked up, and I huddled a little deeper into my jacket.

"You all right?" Garrett asked as we followed Kerr and Cassie.

"Yep. Just hoping that Shax doesn't freak out when he comes home and I'm not there."

Kerr glanced back at me, his gaze meeting mine before dropping to my belly and back up again.

"He will freak out."

Cassie elbowed him.

"That's not what you tell a pregnant woman. They're supposed to avoid stressful situations."

"Then, she shouldn't have left the house."

"But I was hungry, remember?" I added.

He grunted, and Cassie glanced back.

"Shax will understand."

Kerr made a new grunt noise that sounded like it fell into the I-doubt-it category. Ignoring him, I studied the golden glow of the approaching sunset and hoped that Cassie and her family would manage a good night's sleep once we were done dealing with these new problems.

When we arrived at Mya and Drav's place, there was a crowd on the snow-covered front lawn just as Julie had said. Like before, they were yelling stuff that would make a sane person roll her eyes.

"While you're in there making babies, we're starving."

"Where are the supplies hidden?"

"We have rights, too."

I snorted at that remark. The survivors from Whiteman had the right to go outside the wall and find their own supplies. They didn't like that right, though.

The people at the back of the crowd noticed us, thanks to

the sound I'd made, and elbowed their fellow protestors until we had the majority of their attention.

"Contagious my ass," someone yelled.

"I have never claimed to have medical expertise," Cassie said. "Feel free to stop coming to me when something hurts."

That shut the crowd up quickly. People made room for Kerr as he continued forward, splitting the group. Cassie and I followed closely behind with Garrett bringing up the tail. Although the people around us were visibly angry, no one tried to stop us as we moved through their numbers.

When we broke through the crowd, I saw there weren't any fey standing outside this time. I wondered if Drav's roar the last time had actually gotten through to the people gathered that they shouldn't push him too far.

Kerr knocked briefly on the front door then let himself in. Heat enveloped me as I crossed the threshold.

Several other humans and fey already had crowded into the living room. Before I could catch more than the tone of the heated discussion our arrival had interrupted, Drav turned to Cassie.

"Mya is not listening," he said angrily.

"Mya is right here," Mya said. "And you need to stop overreacting."

"Why don't you tell me what's concerning you, Drav?" Cassie said as Kerr helped her from her jacket.

"You said Mya needs rest and food for the baby to grow. She will not eat or rest."

"It's kind of hard to eat when I don't feel well, and I'm not able to rest with all the yelling going on."

"Then let me kill them," he said, his frustration evident.

Mya gave Cassie a look.

"Do you see what I'm dealing with here?"

Drav's eyes narrowed, and he opened his mouth to say more.

"Excuse me," I said, sticking out my hand and purposely interrupting him.

"I'm Angel. I don't think we've officially met. I just wanted to say, thank you for letting me stay here."

Drav's hand closed around mine.

"All females are welcome," he said.

I gave my most angelic smile as I continued to hold his hand and let my gaze drift around the room.

"I don't know everyone here. Will you introduce me?"

He blinked slowly at me then turned to look at Mya.

"It's polite to introduce new people," she said.

He grunted and went around the room.

"This is Jessie and Byllo, Cassie and Kerr, and Eden and Ghua. Those are Tor, Gyrik, Brog, Thallirin, and Merdon."

While I learned names, the distraction helped lower some of the tension in the room. I winked at Mya when she mouthed "thank you" in my direction.

"Are you hungry, now?" Drav asked Mya as soon as he finished the introductions.

"No. We need to stay focused on the immediate problem. The hounds. We were drawing in infected before the hounds because of the lights at night. With the hounds howling for hours on end, more infected are being drawn in. And it's not just here. Tenacity's construction is now moving more slowly than planned because of the constant arrival of new infected."

"We cannot destroy the hearts without Molev," Drav said.

Thallirin and Merdon said nothing from their positions near the kitchen.

"The immediate problem is not the hounds but the humans," Drav said. "They are loud and preventing you from resting."

"This isn't just about me, Drav. Look around. Kerr and Cassie are exhausted. So are Jessie and Byllo. Why do you think that is?"

"The hounds keep the children awake at night," Kerr said. "Each howl fills them with fear. Even Caden, who is too young to know what a hound is."

"Children are smart. They can pick up on the fear of others. That's how Caden knows to be afraid even when he doesn't know what the creature is," Cassie said to Kerr. "He remembers the sound of it from his time trapped in the attic and from Dawnn's reaction to it."

Kerr frowned, and Cassie looked at Drav.

"And while Mya is right that the hounds are an immediate problem—" she looked at Mya "—Drav is right that the survivors from Whiteman need to be addressed, too. And not only because of their noise."

Cassie glanced at me.

"Someone broke into Shax's house and took all the food," I said. Given Drav's current level of aggression at the survivors, I didn't mention the destruction of property.

"It should be easy to find who did it," he said. "We will search every house."

"We can't," I said firmly. "It'll only increase the tension here.

"Someone stole food. We can't allow it to continue," Mya said, agreeing with Drav.

"You won't," I said. "The wall at Tenacity is almost done, right? When everyone goes there, the problem will be solved. Doing something now will only damage the already fragile co-existence we have going on between the fey and the humans." I looked at Drav. "You need women. And, no matter how pig-headed some people are acting, the remaining humans need you. Searching houses will look like an act of aggression."

"How do you propose we deal with this then?" Mya asked.

There was no condescension in her tone, just an open willingness to hear someone else's idea.

"There's a group of people out there focused on the fey as being the big bad evil. Let them know what happened."

"And if they turn on each other, we'll be caught in the crossfire," Jessie said.

"So, don't turn them on each other. Give them rules and consequences. Food was stolen from a house. Anyone caught taking food from a house that is not their own will be immediately removed from Tolerance," I said.

"And I think we can confidently say that the rule will apply in Tenacity, too," Cassie said. "Matt won't abide by stealing."

I agreed with her.

"Along with the rule, we need to give them something," I said.

Mya made a face.

"We've given them plenty, and they've taken more beyond that. I'm not inclined to give even more."

"I know. But the people who took the food did so because of the same problems we're discussing," I said. "The hounds are drawing in more infected, making it harder for people to safely go out for their own supplies."

"With less fey accompanying us, it's getting hairy out there," Garrett said, speaking up for the first time. "I'm willing to pull my own weight and even the weight of a few of the freeloaders. But, I'm not suicidal, and I'd need to be able to keep going out like I have been."

"You see the catch, right? Without anyone going out for supplies, the people will only get more desperate. Telling them they'll get kicked out if they steal while leaving them no option but to face death to get their own food...well, it's the same thing. The hounds need to die."

As soon as I said it, the first howl rang through the air. I glanced at the curtained window, noticing the lack of light around the edges for the first time.

Outside, the shouting got louder. Mya sighed and looked at Drav.

"I know you want to help them, Drav. I do too. But Angel is right. We have to look at the bigger picture. Molev put that rule in place for a reason, just like we're considering putting a rule in place now. But sometimes, circumstances force exceptions to the rule."

"For example, if Mya's hungry and wants to come into my house and help herself to some food, should she be kicked out?" Cassie asked.

"No," Drav and half the fey said immediately. "She is growing a baby and needs food."

"Exactly. Mya's circumstance necessitates an exception to our 'no taking food from someone else's house' rule."

"And our current circumstance necessitates an exception to Molev's rule. With his absence, this group should have the power to witness the destruction of the hearts in his place."

Drav's gaze swept the room then he turned to face Thallirin and Merdon.

"Destroy them."

Thallirin reached for the bag he had slung over his shoulder.

"I'm looking forward to a good night's sleep," Jessie said quietly from the other side of the room. "I think I've picked up a bug or something, feeling this run down."

Byllo's eyes grew big.

"She means we are more likely to get sick when we're exhausted and underfed because our immune systems are weaker," Cassie said before the fey could freak out that a bug was living inside his woman.

Several grunts sounded around the room, and I knew Byllo hadn't been the only fey ready to freak out.

Thallirin withdrew a jagged black rock the size of his

palm from the bag and handed it to Merdon. Something about the rock made me feel wrong. Not sick exactly, but not well either. The stone pulsed with a negative light, a darkness that made me think of deep-seated hate and even deeper fear.

The big fey's scarred fingers closed around the stone, masking some of its darkness. Merdon squeezed hard, his muscles bulging with effort. For several seconds, nothing happened. Then, the rock just disintegrated into black dust. Outside, a howl cut off mid-crescendo.

"Do not dump that on my floor," Mya said.

Drav got Merdon a bag for the dust while Thallirin pulled out the other two hearts. This time, they destroyed them together.

The hounds silenced. The people on the lawn seemed to notice because they quieted, too.

Eden stood suddenly and rushed for the bathroom. Ghua hurried after her with Cassie close behind. In the hush, I heard every choking gag.

"It must be something going around," Jessie said, standing. "I felt like that when I woke up from my nap. A quiet night and a solid eight hours should help everyone."

Byllo helped her with her jacket, and as she lifted her arm, her shirt lifted a little, showing a bruise. I cringed, and she caught my expression as she turned.

She smiled slightly. "I know it looks bad, but it doesn't hurt at all. For the life of me, I can't even remember doing anything that would cause it." She lifted her shirt again to look at it. "I've been so tired lately, though, who knows what I've run into."

Cassie came out of the bathroom and caught sight of the bruise before Jessie lowered her shirt.

"Can I see that again?" she asked.

She gently touched the discolored area.

"Does any of this hurt?"

"Nope."

Cassie glanced at Mya.

"There's no tone of purple or yellow. I don't think it's a bruise."

"You think…?" Mya looked at Jessie with wide eyes.

"Do you have any grey spots?" Cassie asked Eden.

"I've seen every inch of Eden," Ghua said. "Just an hour ago, and there are no grey patches."

"Given both Eden and Jessie's nausea and now this, I think some more tests are in order."

"Tests?" Jessie asked. "What kinds of tests?"

"The pee kind," Mya said.

"Oh, hell no!" Eden called from the bathroom.

"I'll be right back," Cassie said, grabbing her jacket.

"Wait," Garrett said. "Everyone is still relatively quiet outside. If they see you leave and come back with something, they'll think you have hidden supplies somewhere. I think we should talk to the people outside, now, while they're quiet and more likely to listen."

"He's right," Mya said. "Would you be willing to speak with them, Garrett? They would be more likely to listen to one of their own. Drav can go with you to back up what you say."

The room became a lot less crowded after that. Jessie and Byllo went to speak with Eden and Ghua. Drav and Garrett went out the front door while Cassie and Kerr snuck out the back.

Tor, Gyrik, Brog, Thallirin, and Merdon quietly watched me sit near Mya.

"I regret ever thinking this place was boring," I said.

Mya snorted.

"Bet you won't make that mistake again."

"Nope."

"Mya," Tor said. "What is a pee test for?"

"There's several different kinds of tests that require urine. The one Cassie is getting is to test for pregnancy."

Three grunts came at the same time.

"More babies?" Brog asked.

"Maybe. We'll have to wait and see."

"I want babies," Tor said. "Can I listen to your baby, Mya?"

She gave me a flat stare. "Drav discovered he can hear the heartbeat if he puts his ear to my stomach." She turned her head to look at Tor. "But like I told you before, it was really quiet when he did that, and he had to plug his other ear, and he stayed like that for a long time before he heard anything."

"Okay," Tor said, stepping forward.

"That wasn't an invitation. It was a nicely worded refusal."

Tor's expression changed to one of disappointment.

The back door opened, and Kerr set Cassie on her feet.

"Got the tests," she said.

She hurried toward the bathroom and kicked Byllo and Ghua out before closing the door.

CHAPTER SEVENTEEN

"THAT ACTUALLY WENT BETTER THAN I EXPECTED," GARRETT said, shutting the front door behind himself.

Drav strode across the room and looked over Mya as if expecting something to have changed in the ten minutes they'd been outside.

"I'm fine, Drav," she said. She shifted her gaze to Garrett. "Did you think any of the protestors looked or acted guilty?"

"More than half. I don't think they've stolen anything, though, based on the expressions on their faces. But, I'm betting they were thinking of it. Hearing that someone took supplies that I'd gone outside the wall to gather seemed to upset a good number of them. And when I told them the punishment for stealing from here on out, there was barely a grumble. Especially now that a few of the braver folks know they can go out tomorrow and hunt for supplies."

"Good. One set of problems dealt with."

"There's another?" he asked.

"Eden and Jessie might be pregnant," I said.

Garrett's expression grew more serious.

"Pregnancy is good," Drav said. "It means more babies. That is not a problem."

"Spoken like a man," Jessie said, emerging from the bathroom. "And, you're not the one who has to carry the baby for nine months, deal with all the aches and pains and worries, or deliver the baby at the end. There's plenty of problems being pregnant, especially now."

She glanced at Mya.

"Sorry, Mya, I didn't mean…"

"No. You're right. All I'm doing is worrying."

"Pregnant women are supposed to avoid stressful situations," Kerr said.

Mya caught me smothering my grin with my hand but didn't say anything.

"We're not pregnant, by the way," Jessie said.

There were several disappointed faces about the room.

"I know that babies represent the future," Mya said. "But we're not ready for a boatload of babies. Do you really think we can care for them when we can't even care for the adults? Adults are way more independent, and you see the level of self-reliance going on out there. Almost none.

"We're scavenging for supplies. What happens when those run out? We're not self-sufficient. We have no sustainable food force. Everything about being pregnant in this world is stressful. That doesn't mean I'm not happy about the baby. It just means we have a lot of work to do, and instead of focusing on trying to make more babies, we need to figure out long-term care for the people who are here."

The room was quiet for several long moments.

"The radishes Angel planted are sprouting," Garrett said. "Maybe the people who have nothing to do can start marking yards for gardens."

"And I heard a bird this morning," I said. "Maybe the animals are returning."

Ignoring us, Mya watched Drav as he squatted down before her and reached out to stroke her cheek.

"You saw how we lived. We know how to hunt, how to fish, how to farm. Your seasons are new to us, but we will be self-sufficient when the snow melts. There is nothing for you to worry about. You only need to think of eating and resting."

Eden snorted.

"So, the pretty little women only need to concern themselves with being barefoot and pregnant? Hell no. I have way more value than that."

"Yes, you do," Ghua said.

Eden shot him a look.

"More value than a sex toy too, buddy."

He grunted and wisely said nothing more.

"Do we?" Jessie asked. "I mean, other than Cassie's medical knowledge, do any of us have a skill set that helps anything in this world?"

"Brenna does," I said. "She was pretty awesome with her bow on the wall."

"Jessie's right," Mya said. "We don't have skills that are

useful. Yet. But, as Drav pointed out, they know how to hunt. And as Brenna proves, we are capable of learning those skills, too."

Several low growls echoed around the room.

"You'd rather have us not learn how to defend ourselves? To be unable to protect ourselves or the children we have if you're not right there to do it for us?" Her gaze pinned Drav. "You know how quickly things can happen."

He grunted, stood, and looked at Thallirin and Merdon.

"Mya is right."

"Say it again, but slower and sexier," Eden said.

Drav glanced at Mya.

"Ignore her," Mya said. "She wasn't being literal."

Drav glanced at Eden then back to Thallirin and Merdon.

"Mya is right that we need to look at the big picture. We cannot scavenge for supplies forever. All fey are needed to create the safe, self-sufficient homes needed to raise children. You've proven yourselves in my eyes."

"And in mine," Mya said.

"Welcome home, brothers." Drav pressed his forehead to Thallirin's then Merdon's. The other fey in the room moved to do the same. There was a bunch of manly backslaps after that.

"We will continue to hunt hounds," Merdon said when they were done.

"Heal first," Cassie said. "That leg needs time."

"What would you have us do?" Thallirin asked.

"You guys lived outside with the hellhounds for lifetimes

in the caverns, right?" Mya asked. "I'm betting you know a lot about them and how they hunt. Maybe you can teach us."

"Not you, Mya," Drav said.

"Why not?"

"You need to rest so the baby can grow."

"Angel's baby has—"

Her eyes got big, and she cringed before looking at me along with every other person in the room.

"So why does Jessie have a grey spot if she's not pregnant?" I asked.

"I'm not sure," Cassie said, willing to play along.

"Maybe she's been sleeping on Byllo's crystal," Mya said, her eyes locked on me.

"Angel is pregnant?" Drav asked.

"What?" I said shocked. "Why would you even say that? We're talking about serious stuff here. Grey spots are important. We need to figure out what's going on."

Drav tilted his head and studied me, unblinking.

"Did I just short him out?" I asked Mya.

"Not a chance. He's probably trying to see through your clothes," Eden said. "So how far along are you, and who's the baby daddy?"

I made a pained face.

"What? You know they're not going to pretend they didn't hear that."

"She's over six months," Cassie said. "Underfed. And without food because she's staying with Shax and someone took everything he had."

Drav growled low while still looking at me, and Mya reached out to smack him.

"No growling at pregnant people. We don't like it. It's scary."

"It's okay. I know it's not directed at me. And I'm not underfed, just underweight. Shax has been great about getting supplies for me."

"When will the baby come out?" Tor asked.

"Babies come when they're ready. And without a calendar, it's hard to know how much longer this bun will be in the oven," I said, patting my belly.

"Might as well take your jacket off," Mya said.

"Yeah," Eden said. "Show us the goods."

I rolled my eyes but shrugged out of my jacket, baggy outer sweater, and the next two layers of clothing as well. With only my loose t-shirt on, I reached behind me and pulled it tight.

The room stayed quiet as every fey stared at my belly.

"Me first," Jessie said as she stood up. She came over and set her hand on my belly. "Welcome to being touched randomly by complete strangers for the next few months. Unwanted public groping is the gift I bestow upon you."

"Too many fairy tales playing at your house," Mya said with a snort.

"Savvy loves Sleeping Beauty."

"If you're smart, you'll start charging a doughnut a touch," Eden said.

"There's doughnuts?" Jessie and I said at the same time.

"Sounds good, doesn't it? There has to be some out there

somewhere. I'm betting we could put some weight on you real fast that way."

"As the only pseudo-medical professional here, I advise against a diet of sweets. We're not equipped to deal with gestational diabetes."

Through all of our banter, the fey hadn't moved an inch. They continued to stare at my belly, and the ninja decided to put on a show. A small bump protruded on the top of my belly as the baby stretched, and it moved toward the equator before disappearing again.

Ghua, Byllo, Tor, Gyrik, and Brog all moved forward to place their hands on my belly.

Eden laughed as question after question poured from them.

"Does it move often?"

"How many weeks until it moved?"

"When will it move again?"

"Does it hurt?"

Before I could answer, Ghua took his hand from my belly, marched over to Eden, and tossed her over his shoulder.

"I think this means we're going. Night everyone!"

Ghua didn't even stop for her jacket before he was running out the door.

"It is pretty late, and Angel's had a long day," Cassie said.

"Very long. I better get back before Shax comes home and sees I'm not there."

"Not alone," Drav said. "Humans already entered Shax's house and took his food. We cannot lose you."

"No one is going to steal me," I said with a laugh. "If anything, they'd—"

"Don't go there," Cassie warned.

"Right."

Drav frowned at us.

"Not alone," I repeated. "Got it. Garrett will be with me."

Drav's gaze flicked to Garrett. I looked back at my friend and knew he was uncomfortable under the fey's scrutiny.

"Shax trusted Garrett," I said.

Drav grunted and looked at me, his gaze flicking to my belly.

"People are angry. On edge. We would all feel better if you chose two fey to stay with you until Shax returns."

"I will go with Angel," three voices said at once.

The fey with women had stayed quiet, as had Thallirin and Merdon. I glanced at the gruff, fierce pair. Since they'd arrived, I'd rarely seen them. And when I had, it had been glimpses of them standing apart from everyone else. Here, but not really belonging.

"Are you guys busy?" I asked them.

Thallirin averted his gaze, choosing to look at the floor. Merdon blinked at me before answering.

"No. We are not busy."

"Would you be willing to stay with me until Shax gets back?"

Merdon gave a single, curt nod while Thallirin looked up at me. While I considered myself a great interpreter of the subtle nuances of fey facial expression, Thallirin's was completely obscure.

"I think I'll head back to my place," Garrett said. "Let Shax know I did what he asked, okay?"

I grinned.

"Don't worry, chicken. I have your back."

He waved goodbye and let himself out while I started re-layering.

"We better get going, too," Cassie said. "Your mom is keeping an eye on the kids. Hopefully, they slept through that little bit of noise." She looked at Thallirin and Merdon. "Thank you for killing the hounds."

They both grunted, their attention on me as Cassie left.

"Sorry about the slip," Mya said as I zipped my jacket. "Need any food for the road? I have chocolate."

"No, thanks. Unless it's a doughnut. Eden made me hungry for those, now."

Mya chuckled, and I waved goodbye, my two escorts accompanying me out the door. When they tried walking behind me, I paused to wave them forward.

"So, you're excellent hunters?" I asked while Thallirin moved to my right and Merdon stepped to my left.

"Yes," Merdon said.

"Does that mean you know how to make a bow? I'd really like to learn how to shoot one. Brenna made it look so easy."

"Brenna takes too many risks," Thallirin said, his deep voice a rough rasp.

I glanced at him, hearing something in his words. It was

confirmed by his expression. A tiny softening around the eyes and mouth. He really liked her.

"Like what?" I asked, wanting to keep him talking. "When I saw her, she was on top of the wall."

"She retrieves her arrows," he said.

"Well, I won't be on top of the wall for a long time. I don't have the ballast for it," I said, patting my belly. "That means I won't be risking fetching arrows from anything more than a target in Shax's backyard. I promise."

Neither commented.

"Do you talk to Brenna a lot?" I asked Thallirin.

"No."

"Why not?"

"She is afraid of me."

"Are you sure?"

"Yes."

"Well, I think that needs to change. You make me a bow, and I'll talk you up to Brenna."

He blinked at me.

"Talk me up?"

"Yeah. It means I'll point out all your good qualities to her so she won't be afraid of you."

He frowned slightly.

"You will lie to her?"

I laughed and shook my head.

"You fey are so amazing, and you don't even know it. No, I won't lie to Brenna. But, I'll probably tell her things she already knows. You're strong and fast. You're fiercely protective and loyal. You're sweet to women. What's not to like? Add all of that on top of the fact that you're probably our only hope for staying alive in this world, and it's a winning combination."

Thallirin grunted, and I watched his gaze skim the walls. He was thinking of her. I could see his hope equaled his despair in the set of his shoulders. In that moment, I totally understood Mya's matchmaking ways.

"What about you?" I asked, looking at Merdon. "Any girl interest you?"

"No. Most females do not look at us."

"Are you sure? We're good at looking when you're not paying attention to us."

"We always pay attention," Merdon said. "Females only look at us when they want something."

"Ouch. That's a pretty low opinion. We're not all like that."

He grunted, and I studied him for a moment.

"You know that means we're not so different from you then, right?"

Merdon glanced at me.

"Well, you fey are only looking at us females because you want something, too. Pussy and boobies. So why are the females bad, but you're not?"

"I never said we weren't bad."

I looped my arms through each of theirs. They both glanced at me but didn't try to pull away.

"You've been apart from everyone else for so long you've turned a bit cynical, I think. But don't worry. There's a cure. The longer you're with good people, the less cynical you'll become." It wasn't a blatant lie. Humans made other humans cynical. I held out hope that being around the fey would make me less so.

"There are not many good people."

I laughed. "You got that right. But we can change. Get better. Have a little patience and faith."

Ninja kicked again just before I reached the house, and I grabbed Merdon's hand and stuck it up under my jacket.

"Feel that?" I asked.

His palm rested over the kick spot just long enough for the little ninja to do it again.

Merdon grunted, and I reached for Thallirin's hand to do the same. His expression hardened at the first kick.

"That's why you're doing what you're doing," I said. "Killing hounds. Putting up with the occasional stuck up woman. Getting hurt. Someday, some woman will see you for what you are and stop demanding things and start giving them instead. Babies. New life."

A low growl came from the tree to the right of the house, and Shax strode from the shadows. Both men withdrew their hands from under my jacket and faced Shax.

"Okay," I said as he strode forward. "That probably looked bad, but it was completely innocent."

I stepped in front of both men and put my hands up.

Shax moved to go around me, but I sidestepped and blocked him again.

"Seriously. It was no big deal. They all know now. Well, they'll probably all know by morning. And just because people know doesn't mean anything is going to change," I said.

He tipped his head down at me, anger in his gaze. Without looking away, he reached out and hit one of the two with a solid thunk.

"Where is Garrett?" he said as he hit the other one.

"Are you asking them or me? Because this is confusing me. Why are they getting hit for something I did? I was just trying to tell them that girls are good, and you're wrecking the message."

He growled and stepped around me then laid into Merdon and Thallirin with several well-placed hits. Neither tried to hit back.

"They don't need to know girls are good." Thump. "They don't need to feel the baby." Crack. "They don't need to be near you because I left Garrett with you." Grunt.

Shax stopped hitting and turned to look at me.

"Where is Garrett?"

"Given your current mood, I'm not going to tell you where he is."

"He went home," Thallirin said.

"Hey!"

"Angel, get inside." Shax looked at Thallirin and Merdon. "Watch her."

He turned to leave, and I panicked.

"Babies come out of vaginas! Their heads rip us right open. It's bloody, and it hurts, and I'm scared, and I need a hug."

Shax had stopped at the word vagina and turned toward me.

"Are you lying to protect Garrett?" Merdon asked.

"Oh, I wish I were," I said, not taking my eyes off of Shax. The big fey studied me without expression for several heartbeats then walked toward me.

"From your vagina?"

"Yep."

He frowned.

"Caden's head is big, and that hole is very small."

"Yep."

His arms wrapped around me, and he held me gently. I leaned into him, savoring the feel of his hold and the fact that I'd saved Garrett's bacon as promised.

"Will there be a lot of blood?"

I set my hand on his chest and patted.

"That's probably a question for Cassie. When I'm not around. I don't want to freak myself out more than I already have."

I suddenly found myself up in his arms.

"Thank you for keeping her safe," he said to the other two fey.

I looked at them, noting Merdon had a split lip and Thallirin had a darkening eye.

"I'm really sorry, you guys."

"Shax!"

The sound of Hannah's voice made me cringe. All the fey watched Hannah approach, her blonde ringlets bouncing with each step.

"Put me down, Shax," I said softly.

"No." His hold on me tightened.

"What are you guys all doing outside?" she said as she joined us.

"Talking about how babies come out of vaginas," Shax said.

"Did you hear that Mya's pregnant?" I asked.

"Yeah. That's actually why I'm here." She smiled at Shax. "I'm willing to try having your baby. But under one condition. You have to keep me supplied in booze."

My mouth dropped open. There were too many levels of wrong in what she'd just said to count them.

"I do not love you, Hannah," Shax said. "You should leave."

There was no denying how happy those words made me.

"Do you know what having a baby means?" she asked. "Sex, Shax. I'm offering you all the sex you want. You don't have to love me."

"I do not want your baby. I want Angel's."

Hannah's gaze shifted to me, and somehow, I kept the hurt from my expression.

"You're pregnant now, too?"

"From before the quakes," I said. "Thirty to thirty-two weeks. Somewhere in there. Not a fey baby."

"Looks like it doesn't matter."

"I'm sorry. I didn't mean to—"

She waved a hand at me.

"It's okay. Like Shax said. He doesn't love me, and I don't

love him. It would have been an easy way to get a drink in this place."

"You know alcohol is bad for a fetus, right?"

"So are infected, hellhounds, starvation, and freezing to death. It's the world we live in. I'm just trying to make the best of it." She gave an unapologetic shrug. "I'll see you guys around."

"I will walk you home," Merdon said. He looked back at me. "You'll need arrows."

I grinned as Merdon walked away with Hannah then looked at Thallirin.

"I'll keep my end of the deal if you keep yours," I said.

He grunted and left me alone with a growling Shax.

CHAPTER EIGHTEEN

"You made a deal with Thallirin?" Shax asked, the growl still in his voice.

His anger didn't worry me in the least.

"Yep. Thallirin likes Brenna. So, I'm going to talk to her for him. Help him get the girl like I tried to help you." I sighed and snuggled into Shax's arms. "Hannah was right there tonight, offering you everything. Why didn't you take it?"

He grunted and started toward the house. He opened the door, balancing me in one arm, then slammed it behind us.

"On a scale of one to ten, how mad are you?" I asked when he didn't move any further into the room.

"That you left the house? That my brothers know about the baby? Or that you let Thallirin and Merdon touch you?"

"That I didn't help you get the girl. But I think your other concerns should probably be addressed first."

He set me down and unzipped my jacket. His expression

was angry. His movements were stiff. But every touch was gentle.

I reached up and cupped his face.

"Why didn't you go for Hannah?" I asked, unable to help myself.

"I do not love Hannah. I love you, Angel."

My insides did all sorts of happy flips. I wanted to believe him so badly.

"For how long?" I asked.

He blinked at me.

"How long will you love me, Shax?"

"Forever."

"That's probably how long you thought you'd love Hannah, and look at how long that lasted."

"You don't believe I love you?"

"I'm saying I'm afraid to trust it will last. You were so desperate for Hannah. You didn't notice any other females. She was it."

"I noticed you."

"When?"

He tilted his head and studied me.

"When you kissed me. It felt nothing like Hannah's kiss." His thumb brushed over my bottom lip. "Your mouth touched mine and changed my heart. I tried to do what you said. I tried to talk to Hannah, but I didn't want to be the man she wanted me to be. I wanted to be the man you wanted. I didn't tell you how much I wanted to see your breasts or taste your pussy. I kept my desperation in."

"Until the night I had dinner here with Garrett," I said in sudden understanding. "What you said, it was all about me."

"Yes."

"And it was because of our kiss? It has nothing to do with you wanting my baby?"

"I want your baby because it's part of you."

Rising up on my toes, I pressed my lips to his. He held still for only a second before growling and backing me into a wall. My heart thumped hard at the feel of his hands gripping my butt as his tongue thrust against mine. He lifted me up, and I wrapped my legs around his waist. Even with jeans and several shirts between us, the feel of his erection as he pressed into me sent a jolt of pleasure all the way to my toes. Groaning, I slipped my hands into his hair and gave myself over to him.

Distracted by the kiss, I wasn't aware that he'd walked up the stairs until he laid me on his bed.

He broke our kiss to look down at me.

"Forever, Angel. What I feel for you, I've never felt before, and it won't fade or go away." His hand slipped under my shirts and settled on my stomach. "It's not because of the baby, but it does include the baby. You are family." His hand stroked my belly, and I believed him. The look in his eyes conveyed both lust and devotion. It wasn't just the baby he wanted. He wanted me, too.

I reached down and pulled my shirts off in one sweep. When my head cleared the material, he leaned back and studied me.

He set his dark hand against my skin and smoothed his hand upward.

"Wrong direction," I said. "I think you want my pants off."

He grunted and helped me wiggle out of my jeans. In my bra and underwear, I got to my knees and reached for his shirt. He let me tug it off and held still as I looked my fill, marveling at every chiseled ridge and indent.

I ran my hands over his rock-hard abs.

"Not going to lie. This is better than Christmas presents. I've been dying to see you without clothes."

He stood and had his pants around his ankles in a heartbeat. My gaze locked on his hard length jutting from his body. Thick and long, his erection was awe inspiring. The stuff dildo companies tried to create but couldn't perfect. Shax was the real deal, and the idea of him inside of me made me clench in anticipation.

I reached out and wrapped my hand around his length.

He hissed out a breath, and I looked at him…at the tenseness in his jaw and the wide depth of his pupils.

"Are you okay with me just exploring for a bit?" I asked.

He grunted.

Leaning forward, I kissed his flat stomach. He twitched under my lips. I trailed little kisses down further.

His skin jumped and quivered, and his hands settled on my head just as I reached the base of his cock.

"Can I taste you?" I asked.

He made a sound like he couldn't breathe. Smiling, I took that as a yes and dragged my tongue along the length of him.

He started to shake. I cupped his balls and closed my mouth around his swollen dark head, humming as I savored the experience.

The sounds coming from him were almost as good as his taste. Just as I was getting into it, I found myself on my back. He bit my bra, tearing through the fabric at the same time as he ripped my underwear from me. His mouth closed over my breast, and his fingers delved into my folds. He circled my clit once, eliciting a groan from me. Then, he was on top of me, spreading my legs.

At the last second, he froze and looked down at me. His pupils were so large I could barely see the color in his eyes. Sweat beaded his forehead.

I reached between us and closed my hand around the hot length of him.

"Stop," he rasped. "We cannot hurt the baby."

"We won't," I said.

I guided him to my entrance, lifting my hips to press against him. His head glided an inch into me before he jerked back.

"Are you sure?"

"Very. Sex is completely safe while pregnant."

I could see the doubt in his eyes.

"Don't leave me hanging now. Soft or hard. Fast or slow. I don't care how you do it, but I want to feel every inch of this amazing thing sliding into me, Shax."

He growled and pressed forward. I got my hand out of the way and wrapped my legs around his waist. He took his time, inching in a bit at a time. I murmured words of encouragement and struggled to take all of him. He was huge.

Once he was fully seated, I wiggled a little, trying to get used to it.

"Don't move," he said, his voice rough.

"I'm just trying to find the right…" I shifted my hips again and felt the magic moment when he was hitting all the right spots. I arched my butt into the mattress, forcing him to withdraw a bit before bucking upward to fully seat him again.

"That," I panted. "Right there."

He lost it when I moved again. He withdrew and slammed into me, taking me hard and fast. I hit a wall of pleasure, and my orgasm demolished everything.

Shax held me and continued to move relentlessly.

I'd barely recovered when I felt another orgasm gathering.

I wrapped my arms around his neck and held on for the ride of my life.

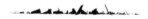

EVEN IN MY SLEEP, I knew life was good, and I smiled myself awake.

Warm and nestled in Shax's arms, I took stock of how I felt. Languid and relaxed. Not sore, thankfully. Definitely educated. Oh, the things the fey enjoyed. I smiled wider and opened my eyes to look at the ceiling. Shax was amazing in and out of bed. Completely perfect.

I thought of what lay ahead of us. The hardship of

surviving in a world with faltering electricity, dwindling food sources, and increasing infected. None of it scared me. Learning to hunt and grow things sounded great. Life was uniquely different. More dangerous in some ways but simpler in so many more.

My stomach let out a little gurgle, and I slipped from Shax's arms before my hunger woke him.

Determined to shower first, I tiptoed to his bathroom and grinned at the large soaker tub. That thing was going to see some use in the upcoming weeks. Knowing I needed to wash my hair, though, I opted for the shower and started unwinding the braid. When I finished, the strands hung below my butt.

While I washed, I remembered the night before. No prior lover compared to Shax in bed. He was all man. Every delicious inch of him. I smiled to myself. Hannah was an idiot, and I was so grateful for it.

The door opened, and I looked over my shoulder at Shax. He paused, spotting me through the glass. As he stared, he grew hard.

"Ready for another round?" I asked.

"Yes."

"I'll make you a deal. You find me something to eat and have it waiting for me in the bedroom, and I'll skip getting dressed and going downstairs to find something for myself."

He walked toward the shower and opened the door.

"I have a better idea." He lifted me up and leaned me against the shower wall, which was thankfully already warmed.

I wrapped my legs around his waist and felt the press of his head against my entrance. I gave a small wiggle and partially seated myself.

"I like your idea better," I said.

His gaze roamed my features, and he reached up, tenderly running his fingers over my wet hair.

"Forever," he said before his gaze met mine.

With infinite slowness, he entered me. My channel stretched to accommodate him, and I felt every delicious bump and ridge. When he filled me completely, he stopped and kissed me hard. I tingled with anticipation, already knowing what would happen.

I ground myself against him.

He growled and pulled his mouth from mine to nibble his way down my throat. One hand cupped my breast and toyed with the nipple.

I rotated my hips again, lifting myself ever so slightly before sliding back home.

He growled and nipped my collarbone. Grinning, I threaded my fingers in his hair.

"You feel so good," I said. "Hot. Hard. Delicious." I gave my hips another wiggle.

A tremor ran through him, and I knew his control was close to breaking.

"You're not an angel," he rasped, lifting his head to look me in the eye.

"Nope. Never have been. That makes me the perfect woman for you, you sexy grey devil. Now, are you going to give me what I want?"

He growled and slowly withdrew. I moaned, waiting for it. Instead of driving into me like I wanted, he eased back in.

I grinned, enjoying his resistance.

"You have amazing eyes. Have I told you that? I love when you watch me. Especially when I was licking your cock last night."

He jerked inside of me, a small hard thrust.

"The way your balls tightened when I did that thing with my tongue...it drove me crazy."

"Me too. Now stop talking."

My grin widened.

"Do you know what I want to lick now?"

"Quiet, Angel. I don't want to hurt you."

I leaned in, my mouth right next to his ear.

"You didn't hurt me last night." I flicked out my tongue and ran it along the tip of his ear.

His control snapped. With a low growl, he withdrew and thrust into me again and again. Even in his frenzy, he was aware. He held me carefully, ended each thrust just before it became too much. I rode the pleasure, tension coiling inside of me.

Clinging to Shax, I let the sensations claim me. My channel clenched, close to release. He growled and thrust a little harder. I felt his shaft swell and jerk. It sent me over the edge, and I came with a loud cry. He jerked within me, his thrust slowing as he found his release a moment later.

His hand stroked over my hair as his hold changed from aggressive to tender.

"You own me," he said, panting in my ear. "Name anything you want, and I will make it yours."

"Your heart. Forever."

"You already have it."

I kissed him softly then wrapped my arms around his neck. He turned us and warmed my back in the water.

Hunger forgotten, I basked in his touch as he washed my hair and soaped my body. His gaze still held wonder at the sight of my breasts. When his hand continued to slide from mound to mound well after I'd said I was clean, I knew we'd be in the shower until the water ran cold.

I didn't get my breakfast for another hour. But I forgave Shax after the third orgasm.

Sitting at the table, I ate the cereal with relish and watched Shax tug on his jacket. It was a new one, the old one having been blood covered and torn from all the infected he'd killed to get us new supplies the night before.

He paused to look at me, his eyes sweeping over my hair, which I'd yet to braid.

"Not even Molev's hair is so long," Shax said.

"Then I'd better put it up again. I don't want Molev thinking I'm more badass than he is."

"No. You are sweet, and your ass is very good."

I snorted.

"I'm going to miss you. Don't take too long."

He grunted and gave me a stern look.

"You will stay in the house, Angel."

"Yeah, probably not. I want to track down Brenna for Thallirin."

He made a sound of frustration.

"But I will promise not to climb the wall to talk to her. I'll keep my feet firmly on the ground."

His expression shifted from "she's not serious" to "she wouldn't, would she?"

He moved toward me and set his forehead against mine, running his fingers through my hair. Even such a simple touch made my breath catch, and my body ache for him.

"Stay safe, my Angel. You are my world."

He kissed me softly then left the house.

I hurried and finished my breakfast so I was only a few minutes behind him. This time, I locked the house despite Shax also having hidden the supplies.

Pausing on the porch, I breathed in the fresh, cold winter air and looked around at the overcast sky. Despite the slightly gloomy weather, the world felt like a brighter, better place this morning. Because of Shax. He loved me. And what I felt for him...I shook my head. I shouldn't feel so deeply already, yet how could I not? That man was incredible. He'd found me marshmallow cereal.

As I walked, I noted there weren't any fey around. When I finally saw one, he nodded to me and glanced at my belly. Word had obviously spread. And not just to the fey. The survivors from Whiteman who were up and moving around weren't as pleasant with their hostile glares and hushed conversation. Their attitudes didn't surprise me. These people had seen my face for weeks. Had heard Matt talk about low blood sugar and had witnessed the extra consideration I'd received. Now they knew the real reason why and were pissed. But, I wasn't worried. No human would lift a finger against me. Not while I was living with the fey who were so enamored with the idea of babies.

I was almost to the wall when someone called my name. I turned and watched Hannah jog toward me. She looked like hell with dark circles under her eyes.

"Morning, Hannah," I said as she approached.

"Morning. Did Shax go out for supplies again?"

A few people slowed on the other side of the street.

"Yep. Did you hear the penalty for stealing supplies?" I asked. I shifted my gaze to the group. "People get banished outside the wall."

"Whore!" one of them called.

"Are we seriously reverting to high school name calling?" I asked. "Use your time more wisely and find supplies, so you don't starve."

I pointed to the ladder.

"Right there's your chance."

"Where do you think we're going? We're not spreading our legs for our supplies."

"Well, there's always the hope you'll come to your senses soon."

Hannah snorted a laugh as the group moved on. Surprisingly, they really did go toward the ladder.

"Do you always take morning walks to taunt the pissed and downtrodden?" Hannah asked.

"It makes my mornings brighter."

She smiled, but the humor didn't last.

"I wanted to apologize for last night," she said.

"Apologize? For what?"

"I knew that Shax had a thing for you and still tried to hit on him, anyway. And right in front of you. It was a shitty thing to do."

"I thought I was doing that to you," I said. "That first day I traded him food for some advice. I was trying to help him win you over, and instead, he won me over."

"He never looked at me the way he looks at you," Hannah said. "It would have never worked between us. I think he knew that but was just being stubborn because I was the first girl who talked to him. Well, excluding Mya."

She looked away for a moment, and I followed her gaze. Merdon stood between two houses. Partially hidden by a tree, he watched us.

"What's it like?" she asked. "Being with a fey?"

"Amazing. Shax is sweet and devoted and so tender."

"Yeah, that's what I thought," she said softly, tearing her gaze from Merdon. "I better get back before Emily eats the last pop tart. Have fun heckling people."

She hurried off, and when I looked back between the houses, Merdon was gone, too.

Hopefully, Hannah wouldn't screw up a second chance. Shaking my head, I started walking along the wall to find Brenna.

CHAPTER NINETEEN

I FOUND BRENNA ON THE OPPOSITE SIDE OF TOLERANCE where infected groaned from the other side of the wall. She stood on top of the barrier with her legs braced apart, firing arrow after arrow.

"What do you do when you run out of arrows?" I asked.

She looked down at me for a moment before resuming her aim.

"Usually, yell for more. If my mom or brother aren't around, one of the fey will get me some."

"Do your arms get tired?"

"Sometimes."

She stopped shooting and turned to look at me.

"Did you need something?"

"Not really. I saw you shooting the other day and wanted to come say hi and thank you. You look pretty amazing up there, and I appreciate what you're doing to keep those of us without skills safe."

"You're welcome. I'm Brenna."

"I'm Angel."

"The pregnant one."

"Yep," I said patting my belly. "I'd say the one and only, but Mya saw what kind of a trendsetter I am and jumped on my wagon, too."

Brenna gave a weak smile. The topic didn't seem to sit well with her.

"Speaking of trendsetters, I should probably let you know that I've asked for a bow, too."

"You did?"

An infected called out, and Brenna glanced over her shoulder.

"Shit," she breathed reaching back for an arrow.

She fired several off in quick succession.

"Everything okay?"

"I don't know. The infected are acting weird."

"Weird how?"

"Like they're purposely doing stuff to get shot." She fired again. "That one was just walking back and forth. Not a lost shamble but like the old shooting gallery decoys. As soon as I shoot one, another one takes its place."

"That does sound weird. Are you the only one watching the wall today? I haven't seen many fey."

She shrugged slightly.

"I think they switched out the ones helping with Tenacity again. Those who aren't sleeping or working there are with the survivors who left for supplies. There always seem to be a few lingering around here, though." Her gaze swept the area around me then narrowed.

I hid my smirk and turned to the east to look for Thallirin.

"Do you see that?" she asked. "At the end of the street."

I squinted and tried to focus on the group walking through the neighborhood. A few split off going to houses on each side. They moved normally, but looked like they'd been through a war. Their clothes were ripped and...I leaned forward as if another two inches would change what I was seeing.

One guy's arm was dangling by a bit of tissue.

"Fuck!"

"Yeah, that's what I thought. Run," Brenna said a moment before she started yelling.

"Infected! Infected are inside! Drav! Infected!"

I ran. Down the road, the group of infected paused as they spotted me. Live prey bolting.

A cry went up. Those going into the houses didn't stop. However, a few of the ones at the front of the group started toward me even as more split off to continue invading houses.

Three fey came running from different directions and converged on the infected. But there weren't enough fey, and the infected weren't the normal, slow ones. And they weren't behaving like normal, either. Instead, they moved like they all had a part in a bigger plan. A distant scream came from one of the houses.

One person down.

I ran harder, breaking my rule and continued to glance

back at the infected coming at me. They'd worked their way up to a sprint.

I swore and made it to the nearest house. The door wouldn't budge. I pounded on the surface.

"Infected are inside the walls. Let me in!"

No one answered. No one came to my rescue.

I looked over my shoulder and saw the infected drawing closer. I'd never make it to the next house. Still, I bolted from the porch and ran for my life. A horn blared from behind me. This time, I didn't look to see if it was working.

I continued northwest, away from the group, running through yards without trying the houses. The stupid break in and people's mistrust was going to get me killed. Slipping and sliding on the snow-covered ground, I thought of the woman who'd tripped on the tent stake and wondered if I'd go out in the same way. And what would happen to the baby when I was bitten. Would it be undead inside of me?

More screaming rang out around the neighborhood. People started to emerge from their houses. I would have tried to warn them to get back in, but I was out of breath. Instead, I ran toward one of the open doors and pushed my way inside.

The woman squawked at me.

"Infected," I panted. "Close the door."

She peered outside instead of listening. I saw a shadow move by her feet at the same time she gasped. Spinning around, I bolted for the back door. Behind me, I heard her strangled cry.

More car horns started to blare, adding to the chaos. I

ran blindly until arms closed around me. I fought until I realized I was being carried, not mauled.

I looked up at Shax's worried twisted face and wrapped my arms around him.

"The houses aren't safe," he said.

I nodded.

He jumped suddenly, landing on the roof of a one-story house and jumped again onto the roof of the two-story house beside it.

"I need to leave you here. Stay safe, my Angel." He kissed me hard and left me on the peak of the snow-covered roof.

Panting and shaky, I stood to see what was happening around me. From my place on the roof, I could see everything. The original group of infected from the east wasn't the only group inside the wall. There were more to the north and the south as well.

Humans ran for their lives amidst the infected. Just below me, Shax grabbed the first human he found and threw the guy onto the one-story roof. He ran for the next human and tossed her onto another roof. It was higher and more steeply pitched. For a terrible moment, I thought she'd slide off; but she managed to grab onto the smoking chimney and hold tight.

While Shax killed infected and tried to get more humans onto roofs, a few brave humans stood against the undead horde and tried to protect others. Two stood back to back, surrounded. One of them was Garrett. I watched in fear as he faced one infected after another, his moves precise and unwavering. But there was so many. He had to be growing tired. Behind him, the other man with short dark hair fought just as fiercely.

"Shax," I yelled. "Garrett needs help."

Shax started working his way toward them, and I scanned the riot of bodies, trying to see where the infected were coming from.

Between the houses, I spotted Drav with Mya in his arms.

"Up here," I yelled, waving my arms. He changed directions and headed my way with two other fey close behind.

Below, Shax reached Garrett and the other man. The three worked together to start clearing their area of the street.

Movement at the wall caught my attention. Brenna stood to the west, waving her hands and pointing. I followed her gaze to where infected were still streaming over the wall. Through the bodies coming up, I saw the ends of a ladder.

Drav jumped to the low first story roof, ignoring the people already there, then to my roof.

"There," I said, grabbing his arm and pointing before he even set Mya down. "The infected are using ladders to get in. We need people on the walls."

The two other fey landed on the roof and deposited Julie and Richard, Mya's parents.

"Stay here, my Mya." He kissed her, just like Shax had kissed me, and jumped down with the other two fey. The group ran toward where I'd pointed. Toward the ladder.

On the wall, the infected weren't just jumping down but fanning out in both directions. I looked at Brenna, the ladder and Drav's group.

"There aren't enough fey," I said, watching the young woman. If Drav went to the ladder first, he would never reach Brenna in time.

She saw the problem, too, because she drew an arrow and began firing rapidly at the infected coming toward her on top of the wall. Her shots were spot-on, but her arrow supply was not limitless.

"Brenna needs help," Mya yelled.

With a roar, another fey jumped up onto the wall and intercepted the horde coming at the young woman. Bodies flew left and right as the infected tried to knock him from their path. None of them stood a chance against Thallirin. Brenna pivoted and started firing at the infected still on the ground.

Seeing her safe for the moment, I focused on Drav's group. The fey plowed through the infected, ripping off heads and tossing them aside. With an impressive coordinated leap, Drav's group landed on top of the wall. They moved quickly, knocking infected to the outside without bothering to remove their heads. Any ladders they found they threw inside so the infected couldn't get back in.

"Where in the hell did they get all those ladders?" Mya asked.

"I hope they're not making them," Julie said with a shiver. Her husband wrapped his arms around her.

"I'm sure they're not, Julie," he said, rubbing her arms. By the look on her face, she didn't believe him, either.

With the ladders removed, the tide began to slowly change. More infected parts littered the streets than infected walked around. Exhausted humans kept fighting beside the fey until there wasn't a single infected left standing. At least, not where we could see.

Shax jogged over to our house along with Garrett and the other man.

"You must stay on the roof until we check the houses," Shax said. "It's not safe yet."

"We're fine up here," Mya called back. "Don't you worry about us."

I nodded.

"Mom? Dad? You okay?" the dark-haired man called.

"We're fine, Ryan," Richard said. "Are you all right?"

"Yeah. No bites thanks to Garrett."

"These infected seemed a lot smarter," Mya said. "Their eyes. The way they moved."

"Yeah, I think the infected were purposely drawing Brenna's attention to the west just before they attacked," I said.

"Are you saying they had a plan?" Garrett asked.

"They were using some of their number as decoys so the rest could get in. You tell me."

"They're evolving. I wish I knew what that meant," Mya said softly. "And what they are evolving into."

Before Shax could move away to start checking the nearby homes, a roar filled the air.

"Mya," a voice called loudly.

"Here," she yelled back.

A fey came running with a woman in his arms. I recognized Ghua and Eden as he drew closer, carrying her.

"Tell him to stop," Eden yelled.

"What's going on?" Mya asked.

"I've been bitten."

Yelling started from the one-story roof next to us.

"Kill her before she turns."

"Put her outside the wall."

Shax snarled at them all, and they silenced.

Shax stopped Ghua when he reached the lawn of the two-story home on which Mya and I waited.

"She needs help," Ghua said.

"There is no help," Shax said. "You know this."

Ghua looked down at Eden, his anguished gaze echoed by his low moan of denial.

"No. Eden cannot become stupid. She is smart and beautiful." He held her more tightly against his chest. "Do not leave me."

Eden lifted a hand and set it against his cheek.

"You are the best thing to have happened to me, Ghua. I'm so glad I didn't shoot you."

Julie sobbed softly behind me.

Kerr came running up with Cassie in his arms. The hope in Ghua's expression as he lifted his head broke my heart.

"Set me down," Cassie said. "I need to check her." Kerr hesitated.

"Hold Eden's head, Ghua, so she cannot bite my Cassie."

Ghua set Eden on her feet and gently cradled her head between his hands. Only then did Kerr put Cassie down.

I watched Cassie lift Eden's clothes, inspecting her skin.

"What are you doing?" Ghua asked. "Her bite is on her hand."

"She's checking for gray marks," Mya said.

"There aren't any," Eden said. "Ghua and I have been watching for them. Nothing. Not even a small bruise."

Eden spontaneously threw up, barely missing Cassie. Cassie backed away, a knowing look crossing her features as Eden groaned in pain and clutched her middle.

There wasn't a survivor alive who hadn't already seen what was happening. We all knew what a bite meant. What we would become in only a few minutes. People learned to say goodbye quickly because, once the vomiting started, there wasn't time left.

Ghua picked her back up, his anguish on his face as he rocked her.

Drav came jogging up.

"Half our number is needed on the wall to keep this from happening again. The other half needs to check the houses for remaining infected. I need one volunteer to run to Tenacity. We need our brothers to return home."

He looked at Ghua and set a hand on the man's shoulders.

"I will take Eden for you."

The pained noise that came from Ghua tore me apart. He held her closer.

"We will leave," he said. "She will keep her head."

She reached up and set her bloody hand on his face.

"Then let's go, big guy. Before I hurt someone." She cried out and convulsed in his arms. A weaker man would have dropped her. Whatever caused her to shake, stopped. Her head lolled back, her eyes open.

"Put me down so I can check her," Cassie ordered.

"No." Kerr stepped back further.

"Drav, hold her head. Kerr, put me down or you're going to be the next one bitten."

Drav held Eden's head, and Kerr set Cassie down. Mya's hand closed around mine and pulled me back. It wasn't until that moment that I realized I'd been edging closer to the roofline.

"There's no pulse," Cassie said.

The people on the lower roof started up again, demanding the fey remove Eden's head.

Ghua roared his rage and pain, and Eden jolted in his arms.

Kerr yanked Cassie back.

"I love you, Ghua, but you're going to make me deaf," Eden said.

"No way," Mya said softly behind me.

I sipped the hot chocolate and listened to the conversation. Eden, Cassie, Mya, Jessie, and I sat in Mya's living room. Byllo was with Julie and Richard at their house with all the kids. More fey had arrived from Tenacity to sweep through the homes in Tolerance and find any hiding infected.

"I don't know about you, but the kids are sleeping with me tonight," Jessie said.

"Same here," Cassie said. "I've seen first-hand how the infected like to hide."

"Grey patch or not, I don't feel as safe in here anymore," Mya said.

"In the house or in Tolerance?" Eden asked.

"Both. You still feeling okay?"

"My hand hurts like a bitch, but my stomach's fine now, and my head stopped throbbing." She looked at Cassie. "Any ideas how I'm not a flesh-craving shambler?"

Cassie shook her head.

"None. We thought it was Mya's exposure to the crystal that made her immune."

"First the grey patches then the immunity," Mya said.

"As much as I hope this grey patch means I'm immune, I really don't want to test it," Jessie said.

"If not the crystals, then what? It has to be something we have in common," Eden said, looking at Mya. "And the test and this—" Eden tapped her arm, "—make it very unlikely that I'm pregnant."

"Birth control?" Cassie asked.

"Yep. Put in just a few weeks before the quakes."

A fey's raised voice coming from outside drew our attention. I turned and pulled back the curtain a bit so we could see what was going on. Brenna was still outside the house with her bow, a layer of protection in case any infected were still lurking. Thallirin stood before her, one arm held out and pointed toward the house.

Several of us inside the house groaned.

"Why do they think they need to be so bossy?" Eden said.

"Ghua only tried that a few times before he figured out it wouldn't end well for him."

We watched Brenna turn toward the house. Her face was pale, and her eyes filled with fear.

"Thallirin needs to take a different approach with her," Mya said. "He'll never win her over this way."

"I don't think she wants to be won over," Jessie said.

Brenna reached the door and let herself in. When she saw us all looking at her, she paused.

"Thallirin sent me in here," she said.

"Did you tell him to stick an arrow up his ass?" Eden asked.

Brenna shook her head and quickly closed the door.

"You should have," Eden said. "Their expressions are priceless when you shock the hell out of them."

"Come join us," Mya said, patting the cushion beside her. "We're trying to figure out why Eden's immune."

"Since arriving at Tolerance," Cassie said, addressing Eden, "have you and Mya spent a lot of time together?"

"Please. Ghua barely lets me out of the house. My vagina is his new shiny toy, and he's not done being in love with it yet."

"Tell me about it," Jessie said. "Byllo is constantly putting on movies for the kids and pulling me away for some play time. We were almost busted four times yesterday."

"Four?" I asked in disbelief. I thought Shax's fascination last night had been because it was the first time. "How many times a day are they after you?"

"Four," Cassie said. "Easily."

"Six," Eden said. "Ghua can manage seven, but I had to tell him he was going to break his happy place if he kept that up."

Cassie frowned slightly. "What we all have in common is the copious amounts of fey semen we are receiving."

Everyone was silent for a moment.

"Are you saying their sperm is like a vaccine against infection?" Mya asked.

"Well, that's sure going to make them popular with the ladies," I said.

"Oh, shit," Eden groaned. "Ghua's going to break his toy trying to protect it."

I laughed along with the rest of the women and thought of Shax. Like many of the other fey, he was out there looking for infected and securing Tolerance. Although I knew he could kill an infected with ease, I still worried about him.

Mya caught me glancing out the window.

"How are things going with Shax?" she asked.

"Good."

"Good or really good?" Eden asked.

I smiled, unable to help myself as thoughts of last night filled my head.

"Really good."

Mya grinned and subtly nodded her head toward Brenna, who was still looking pale but listening.

"It turns out he and I were both pretty thickheaded. I thought he wanted Hannah. Then, when he didn't anymore, I thought he only wanted me for the baby. It turns out, he wants me for me, which is perfect. The man is built like a horse," I added.

Mya and Eden both gave little shakes of their head as Brenna paled.

Ignoring them, I looked at Brenna.

"Speaking of built men, I saw Thallirin jump on the wall to help you. I'm glad he was there."

She nodded.

"Why are you afraid of him?" I asked.

All subtle movement stopped.

Brenna looked down at her hands.

"It's not just him," she said. "I don't like to be touched."

"Then, tell him that. If there's one thing I learned while getting to know Shax, it's that open, clear communication is key. Plus, you're way too badass to meekly scurry into the house with the pregnant womenfolk when he points. That kind of reaction will give the fey all kinds of crazy ideas."

"Yeah. Like we'll suddenly start listening to them," Eden said with a snigger.

The door opened, and Drav stepped in.

"The houses are clear, and Matt is on his way."

CHAPTER TWENTY

I walked with Mya and the rest of the women toward the entry circle. Drav had said that many of the other survivors were already there. Those who weren't, we saw along the way. Carol and Harry's heads were on the ground near their house, the door broken in and marked with a bloody handprint.

Garrett was standing near them, looking down. I broke away from the group and went to him.

"Hey," I said. "Are you okay?"

He exhaled heavily.

"Yeah. For all the trouble Carol and Harry caused, I never wanted this to happen."

"No one did."

I reached for his hand, but a low growl stopped me.

"No touching Garrett," Shax said from just behind us.

Garrett paled, but I grinned and turned around.

"I'd kiss you to prove you have nothing to worry about, but you have a little blood on you."

He didn't have a little. Shax was covered in blood from head to toe. It plastered his clothes and matted his hair. Garrett was spotless. Based on his wet hair, I figured he'd just come from showering.

"Are the rest of your housemates okay?" I asked him.

"Yeah. They're inside."

"Did you know these people?" Shax asked.

"These are two of the people who lived with me."

"The people who ate Angel's food?" Shax asked.

"Yep. The very same," I said.

Shax growled low.

"There's no point in that anymore, Shax. They're dead."

He grunted and looked down the street where Mya and the others were walking.

"You should stay with them. It's safer."

"No, it's safer with you and Garrett. Besides, why do we need to go to the wall anyway?"

"Matt is coming. He will take the survivors to Tenacity."

"That still doesn't answer why I have to be there."

"You will help decide who can stay." Shax looked at Garrett and crossed his arms.

"Crap," Garrett said under his breath.

"You know I'm going to vote for Garrett to stay, right?"

Shax grunted, and I reached for Garrett's hand again, despite Shax's warning growl.

"Is Drav your brother?" I asked.

"Yes."

"By blood? Do you have the same mother and father?"

"I do not know."

"And if you did know, would you still call him your brother even if he wasn't related by blood?"

"Yes."

"And the baby I'm carrying? Will you call this your child even though you didn't help make it?"

He frowned, another low warning growl emanating from him.

"I really wish you'd stop annoying him," Garrett said softly.

"I'll take that as a yes," I said to Shax. "So, then you'll understand how I feel about Garrett. He's like a brother to me."

Shax studied Garrett.

"Do you want to be her brother?"

Garrett's hold on my hand changed. Where I'd been the one keeping the connection before, now he was.

"I'd like that a lot."

Shax uncrossed his arms with a long exhale.

"You can be Angel's brother like Ryan is Mya's brother. You will help me protect Angel."

"I will," Garrett said.

Shax grunted. "You can stay."

I grinned and started dragging Garrett toward the rest of our group.

"Come on, let's go talk about your citizenship."

When we arrived, the group of women from Mya's house gathered in a cluster. The survivors stood near the wall. It was sad to see the number so greatly reduced. But, there was no taunting or yelling this time. Too many had been lost for the hatred to push its way through the grief.

A rumble outside the wall brought many of the people out of their shell-shocked stupors.

Brenna, who stood on the wall under Thallirin's watchful eye, called out.

"Matt Davis is here with the trucks."

Fey came leaping over the walls, the number of them swelling and outnumbering the survivors. One of the fey brought Matt over and set the man on his feet.

Matt's gaze swept over the crowd and found Mya and Drav. He walked up to them and spoke loudly so everyone could hear.

"I'm sorry it took so long. Thank you for housing my people and keeping them safe."

"Safe?" someone yelled. "Look around you."

Matt did, his gaze flitting over the infected bodies nearby and a few of the survivor bodies further away before he faced his people.

"Whiteman wasn't safe. With each breach, we were losing more and more of our number. We couldn't stay there. Mya and Drav willingly offered the use of Tolerance as a refuge for us while we started building Tenacity. Since you entered these walls, Mya and Drav have been sending me updates daily, and I've been doing the same.

"The losses we have suffered today are tragic and should be viewed as a lesson.

"The fey, alone, cannot keep you safe. Walls alone cannot

keep you safe. You alone cannot keep your loved ones safe. The only way we will ever have a chance is if we stop segmenting ourselves and start working together as a united front to face the infected.

"I look around at those who have fallen, and I feel deep sorrow for those they've left behind and humanity as a whole. Our numbers are dwindling. We can try to find fault, or we can take responsibility. One will see the end of us and one might just save our race."

He turned to Drav and Mya and indicated the crowd.

"Your turn," he said.

Mya stepped forward.

"Matt's right. It's time to set differences aside and start living together for a better future. But, we're not going to force a peace you don't want. Those who want to leave and live at Tenacity can head for the ladders. However, know that there will be no fey there to guard the walls they helped build. That is on you. And supplies will not be delivered like before. That is on you, too."

Several outcries were made, and Matt raised his hands.

"The fey will go on supply runs daily, and anyone who needs food is welcome to go with them and gather what they need. There will be no handouts. We don't own the fey, and they owe us nothing."

"And if we stay here they'll guard the walls and keep giving us supplies?" an angry voice asked. "Is this your way of trying to whore more of us out?"

"No," Mya said. "Those who want to stay will need to prove they know how to live with the fey. People who use them and their generosity and give nothing in return will not be welcome here."

"Some of us aren't willing to sleep with a fey to get their help," another voice said.

"I can't believe you assholes are still judging," Eden said. "Did you not see what happened? Those of us sleeping with the fey appear to be immune to infected bites."

Matt glanced at Mya.

"Is that true?" he asked.

"Eden was bitten and didn't turn. Female survivors not having physical relations with the fey were bitten and did turn."

"I believe it might have to do with fluid exchange," Cassie said.

"Bring on the baby batter," Emily said under her breath.

"Is it true?" someone asked.

"This is bullshit. They're just trying to make us sex slaves?"

"What about the men? I ain't into dudes but have no problem with the fey."

Matt raised his arms again to quiet the crowd for Mya.

"This information isn't a ploy to force relationships. We don't even know if it's true or not. It's speculation."

"And not something we're willing to test on others," Cassie said clearly.

"You have a decision to make," Matt said loudly. "Tenacity or Tolerance. Both have rules. Stealing supplies will get you booted from either place.

"If you want to stay at Tolerance, you need permission

from Mya and the other women. If you want to stay in Tolerance, you accept their housing assignments which very well could be with one of the fey. You will not need to go on supply runs if you stay at Tolerance, but you will need to pull your weight."

"If you want to stay in Tenacity, Matt will welcome anyone," Mya said. "Like in Tolerance, you will need to pull your weight. Matt will continue to assign duties based on your capabilities. Unlike in Tolerance, you will be allowed to choose your own living companions."

Grumbles started when she finished.

"Or you can strike out on your own," Drav said loudly. "No one is forcing you to choose either place."

"There's the ladder," Mya said, pointing.

People who wanted to stay approached our group. Most of them were women with a few men thrown in. The married couples were assigned to stay with a fey on a probationary basis. Single women were assigned a fey roommate at random. It was like Christmas for the fey.

The majority of the survivors went to the trucks.

Matt came over to talk to me since I didn't have much input for the group when deciding who should stay.

"How are you?" he asked.

"Good."

"Heard the cat's out of the bag."

"It is. The fey are in love with the idea of babies, so it's not as bad as I'd thought it would be."

"And this one?" Matt asked, nodding to my right.

I glanced over and saw Shax striding my way with a scowl

on his face. He was clean and wearing shorts and nothing else.

"That one loves me," I said with a smile.

When Shax reached me, I stood on my toes to press my lips to his.

"And I love him, too," I whispered.

SWEATY AND SATED, I LAY IN SHAX'S ARMS. OUTSIDE, I HEARD the low rumble of a plane passing overhead and jumped out of bed.

"Come on. Let's go."

"They still need to land and return here with news," Shax said, not getting out of bed. "We have time."

"Not if you want to help me shower," I turned my back to him and exaggerated my walk on the way to the bathroom.

His hands cupped my breasts before I reached the shower. Once he'd learned that he had the cure to infection, he'd been doing his best to vaccinate me. And I was loving it.

Thirty minutes later, I was dressed and sitting at the table when Garrett let himself in.

"Did you hear it?" he asked, pulling up a chair.

In the days since the infected break-in, Garrett had grown more comfortable around Shax. The other fey were treating him like another Ryan, too. A helpful human male to be protected. There weren't many who could claim that status.

"Yep. That's why I managed to sneak out of bed."

"If you start going into details again, I'm leaving without you," Garrett said.

I grinned.

"All I said at the last meeting was that Shax needed more clothes. Dawnn's the one who said the fey's equipment matched their height, and the pants you get on supply runs need to be loose enough or the whole world's going to know which way they hang."

"Then you and Eden started comparing which way your men hung. It's not something a brother should hear. Back me up on this one, Shax," he said as Shax walked into the room, wearing loose-fitting athletic shorts.

"Why does hearing about my cock bother you? It does not bother me to hear about Ghua's cock or how he uses it to get Eden to say funny things. Sharing stories is how you learn."

Garrett dropped his head into his hands in defeat while I laughed my ass off.

"You should come with me to talk to Ghua," Shax said. "Maybe you can learn something, too."

"Nope. I think I'll stick with Ryan and focus on supply runs. Are you going to finish that cereal or keep laughing?" Garrett asked me.

I quickly drank my milk and got my jacket on. Together, the three of us went to Mya's house where the rest of the couples were already gathered.

It didn't take long before a fey and a human also arrived.

"Any news?" Drav asked.

Although Whiteman's base no longer housed humans, a few fey continued to guard the remaining planes, the only means we had of monitoring the world beyond the borders of the supply runs.

"We spotted several signs of survivors to the west. Vehicles driving and groups of infected gathered not far behind them. We kept our distance from the vehicles but used the plane to distract the infected. We've given Matt the coordinates so the next search party can check it out."

"But no sign of Molev?" Mya asked.

"No," the fey answered.

The group was quiet.

"Then we keep searching," I said.

"And until we find him, we'll continue what we've been doing," Mya said. Around the room, everyone agreed.

Since the break-in, we'd decided to stop surviving and start living. Granted, we lived in the eye of an apocalyptic storm. There was no denying that. But we were embracing it. The supply runs were for more than just supplies, now, and they were equally manned with fey and humans. What we needed to make Tolerance and Tenacity self-sufficient havens was almost complete.

We just needed spring to arrive. I set my hand on my belly, a sense of anticipation building. I couldn't wait for the next step in our journey.

Spring would be a new beginning all around.

THANK you for reading Demon Night! Want to know as soon as the next one is ready? Sign up for my newsletter at MJHaag.melissahaag.com/subscribe!

AUTHORS NOTE

Thank you for reading Demon Night! Angel's story was just too fun to write, and I'm excited to dive into the next story. But who to choose? There's the question of where Molev went, Thallirin's hopeful interest in Brenna, and whatever's going on between Hannah and Merdon. Not going to lie... that last one is brewing up to something intriguing.

While we wait for the next story to finish mentally percolating, I'll be expanding another world I've created. That's right! That Beastly Tales will not be the only fairy tale retelling after 2019. Watch for the Tales of Cinder this summer. It'll be dark and full of conflict and sex and maybe some conflicting-sex. We'll just have to wait and see on that one. I'm still writing. ;)

If you want to keep up to date on what I'm working on, sign up for my newsletter at mjhaag.melissahaag.-com/subscribe or join my facebook fan group, MJ's Curvy Cartel. Hope to see you there!

INSIDE SCOOP

Did you know that I write under another name? I do! Check out these books by Melissa Haag (also me).

Hope(less)
(perfect for readers who love shifters and swoon worthy heroes)

Being a human, Gabby didn't count on meeting a silent, ruggedly-handsome werewolf with a single-minded determination to make her his mate. When she tries to run, he's not the only one to follow. Something truly dangerous is after her, and Gabby must turn to Clay for help if she ever hopes to discover who is hunting her for the secrets she's spent her whole life protecting.

Fury Frayed
(perfect for readers who love mythology, a multitude of shifters, and heroine badassery)

Abandoned in a town of mythological creatures, Megan must discover why she's part of a world she never knew existed and who is killing humans before she becomes the next victim. Her only consolation is the shy guy hot enough to melt the pants off a popsicle. Bring it.

SERIES READING ORDER

Resurrection Chronicles

Demon Ember

Demon Flames

Demon Ash

Demon Escape

Demon Deception

Demon Night

*More to come!

Also by M.J. Haag

Beastly Tales

Depravity

Deceit

Devastation

Tales of Cinder

Disowned (Prequel)

Defiant

Disdain

Damnation

Connect with the author

Website: MJHaag.melissahaag.com/

Newsletter: MJHaag.melissahaag.com/subscribe

Lightning Source UK Ltd.
Milton Keynes UK
UKHW011827140420
361682UK00007B/2092